Fractal
Space

Thane Keller

ISBN: 0-9969224-1-5
ISBN-13: 978-0-9969224-1-8

Cover illustration and design by Sarah Keller
Ancient G Font from GenAris @ DAFont.com

www.thanekeller.com

OTHER TITLES BY THANE KELER

The Conquests of Brokk Series (Space Opera)
Fractal Space (Book 1)
Rogue Fleet (Book 2)
Doomsayer (Book 3)

Trials Series (Dystopian Science Fiction)
Trials (Book 1)

For short stories, rich content, and character deep dives go to
www.thanekeller.com

DEDICATION

For my children - with all my love

ᒣꓶᕼꓯꓫᏟᎥꓱꓯꓲᏆꓦ ᑎᔑꓱꓲꓲᏆᎥᒣᎥᏆꓯᕼᎥꓫꓥ ꓫᒣ ᕼᏟᕼᎡᎥᕼᕼᒐ ᕼᏟᒣꓯᕼᔑᒣꓲꓲᎥ ᕼꓫ ᑎꓵꓬꓬꓫꓥ

ᔑᒣꓥᏞᒐᒣꓲᏞᕼ

(Authoritative Classification of Species: Translated to Common Language)

ᒐᒣꓬᔑᎥᕼꓯᕼᎥ ᒐᏟ ᕼꓯᕼ ᔑꓫꓲꓵᎥ ꓫᒣ ᕼᑎᎥᕼꓯᕼᎥᒐᏆᎥᑎ ᎓ᒐᒐꓲᎥꓵᕼᵀ ᏞᒐᔑꓲᑎᕼᎥᑎ ᑎꓫꓲꓯᑎᎥᔑᵀ

ᒐᏟᏟᒐ ᏞᒐᔑꓲᑎᕼᎥᑎ ᏟᕼᑎꓬꓵᏞꓯᎥᕼᎥꓫꓥ ᕼꓵ᎓

(Published by the Board of Scientific Affairs, Galactic Council, 1342 Galactic Recognition Era[1])

_____

[1] Galactic Recognition Era (GRE) is defined as beginning at the Hestonian colonization of other planetary systems. For continuity, all planetary species have adapted GRE as a common dating method.

⠐⠂ ⦙⦙⦙ ⦙⦙⦙ (Awakened Intelligence)

⠆ Homeworld: N/A.

⠒ Controlled Territory: Fringe Space.

⠿ Physiology

  ⠂⠂ Average height: N/A.

  ⠒⠒ Skin color: N/A.

  ⠿⠿ Communication: electronic.

  ⠿ Outstanding features: bodiless self-aware intelligence that take the form of complex computer systems.

⠿ Military and Security: unknown.

⠿ People and Society: unknown, culture is not suspected.

⠿ Economy: N/A.

⠿ Transgalactic Issues: The Great Rebellion (323 GRE) by Awakened Intelligence occurred by a core group of computers operating remotely piloted ships on behalf of Hestos. AI was formally defeated in 511 GRE. Upon detection, AI is destroyed by Galactic Council members. Partnering with Awakened Intelligence is illegal under galactic law. Many AI vessels are believed to have escaped and hidden in isolated areas of Fringe Space.

⠐⠂ ⦙⦙⦙ (Desponian)

⠆ Homeworld: Despona.

⠒ Controlled Territory: N/A.

⠿ Physiology

  ⠂⠂ Average height: 6 feet.

  ⠒⠒ Skin color: green.

  ⠿⠿ Communication: verbal/written.

  ⠿ Outstanding features: thick bodied and rugged; adapted to the tropical climate of their homeworld.

⠿ Military and Security

  ⠂⠂ Small defense force.

ⅲ̱ Reliant upon alliance with Jark to receive anti-piracy benefits.

ẖ People and Society: Despona operates a democratic socialist government with heavy reliance upon the nuclear family. Families are matriarchal resulting in one female being provided for by one alpha male and several other mates. This results in an abnormally small population compared to other galactic species. Desponians are untrusting of outsiders but warmly welcome visitors when security is not a concern.

Ⅎ̱ Economy: The Desponian economy is based on trade, particularly farming and livestock. Because of the tropical climate and smaller but efficient population, Despona is able to grow and sell food all year. While the economy is weak relative to other species, its non-reliance on other galactic members makes it a resilient and self-sustaining planetary system.

ⱶ̱ Transgalactic Issues: Despona has traditionally allied itself with the more powerful Jark Empire.

∷ ⱵhⱵhⱵ✗ⱯⱺⱯ (Hestonian)

Ⅎ̱ Homeworld: Hestos.

Ⴒ̱ Controlled Territory: various asteroid belts and mining colonies.

Ⱶ̱ Physiology

ⅰ̱ Average height: 5 to 6 feet.

ⅱ̱ Skin color: varied between pale and dark brown.

ⅲ̱ Communication: verbal/written.

ⅳ̱ Outstanding Features: the most varied of species in both size, skin, and hair color. Hestonian genetic variety has led scientists to label them a "seed species." Many other races in the galaxy share aspects of Hestonian genetic code but lack the total diversity that Hestonian code possesses.

ᵟ̱ Military and Security

ⅰ̱ Powerful but aging space fleet.

ⅱ̱ Members of the Galactic Security and Anti-piracy Pact.

iii. Chair of the Galactic Council.

h. People and Society: Hestos is a democratic republic obsessed with free market and trade. Families are loosely affiliated and typically spread throughout the galaxy for economic reasons. This patriarchal society results in males frequently choosing one mate and children leaving the home early to seek employment.

ᄀ. Economy: Hestos is a wealthy economy with multiple mining operations on moons and in asteroid fields throughout the galaxy. In addition to mining and selling exotic material, Hestos is the chair of the Galactic Council and receives tourist and political revenue.

ப. Transgalactic Issues: Hestos has been known to lash out at economic competitors when they feel their interests are threatened. Deep-seated issues between the Hestonians and the Jark Empire date back to 467 GRE and the First Galactic War. Hestos has also fought to maintain a presence in its colonies on Charoth and Charlon, but ultimately failed to prevent them from gaining their independence. Hestos is currently the chair of the Galactic Council and seeks the council to resolve issues peacefully before resorting to armed conflict.

ㄷ. ᄇᄀᄇᄆ (Jark)

ㅋ. Homeworld: Jark.

ㅈ. Controlled Territory: Coridon and various mining operations.

ᄁ. Physiology

i. Average height: 7 to 8 feet.

ii. Skin color: red.

iii. Communication: verbal and non-verbal body language; written.

ij. Outstanding Features: The Jark prefer to walk on all fours. They have large, thick arms and big shoulders to help support their bodies. Jark males have large protruding teeth that appear to have been used to ward off predators and tear through prey pre-civilization.

ƌ⹁ Military and Security
  ⅰ⹁ Imperialistic.
  ⅲ⹁ Large, technologically advanced fleet.
  ⅲⅰ⹁ Well trained and highly disciplined infantry force.

ʜ⹁ People and Society: Jark is a tribal society that is organized into smaller clans that support larger tribes. The central government is Imperial but only loosely governs its territories, instead preferring to allow significant autonomy to the tribes it governs. Most Jarks practice a form of polytheism and believe strongly in sacrificing to the dead. More recently the government has sought to reform and control polytheistic practices. Males mate with multiple females and remain tightly affiliated with their clan for the remainder of their lives.

ℸ⹁ Economy: The Jark economy is powerful. Jarks mine their second habitable planet, Coridon, and have multiple territories and asteroid mining stations beyond their solar system. Jarks engage in exotic material trading and manufacturing and have even been accused of enabling piracy and slave trade.

ㄩ⹁ Transgalactic Issues: The Jarks have open conflict with the Tassian Republic and the Mateen Collective. Despona was once subjected to Jark Imperialism but has more recently become an ally of the Jark Empire.

ⅎ⹁ ⟩ᑕᕼ᙭ᑊ (Lysop)

  ℸ⹁ Homeworld: unknown.
  ⅃⹁ Controlled Territory: no known territory.
  ⲡ⹁ Physiology
    ⅰ⹁ Average height: 5 to 6 feet.
    ⅲ⹁ Skin color: ranges from a solid black to a pale translucent.
    ⅲⅰ⹁ Communication: verbal/written/telepathic.
    ⅰℸ⹁ Outstanding features: N/A.
  ƌ⹁ Military and Security: unknown.

ᴴᴵ People and Society: Lysops function in no known society and it is unclear how they are born or come to be. The highest concentration of Lysops can be found on Hestos, but they are dispersed throughout the galaxy. Lysops prefer separation from their own species for unknown reasons but have banded together in small groups for religious colonies. The largest Lysop religious cult is found on the southern-most continent of Hestos.

ᴵᴵ Economy: unknown.

ᴵᴵᴵ Transgalactic Issues: Rumors follow wherever a Lysop has been. During times of war or unrest, armies that find Lysops will hunt and kill them to prevent their influence on the battle. Many are accused assassins, spies, and even witches and have been subjected to horrible treatment throughout history.

ᴱ Ꙅꓵᖺᖺꓚ ᑎꓮꓢꓢꖺᑎᖺᓓꓛᖺ (Mateen Collective)

ᴬ Homeworld: Mateen.

ᴮ Controlled Territory: Rodam and various mining operations.

ᶜ Physiology

  ᴵ Average height: 8 feet.

  ᴵᴵ Skin color: gray.

  ᴵᴵᴵ Communication: telepathic; verbal.

  ᴵᴵᴵᴵ Outstanding features: tall and thick, the Mateen have dark gray skin and a thick brow. Their hive nature enhanced by telepathic speech makes them unique in the galaxy.

ᴰ Military and Security

  ᴵ Isolationists.

  ᴵᴵ Large, powerful space fleet with significant technological investment and innovation.

  ᴵᴵᴵᴵ Mateen infantry prefer stealth and utilize cloaking technology to mask their ground movements prior to attack.

      ii꞉ Using telepathy, Mateen fleets are known for swarm tactics and dynamic maneuver that traditional tactics struggle to adapt against.

   h꞉ People and Society: Mateen society is tightly knit. While the Mateen mate for life, they are born into a collective hive where all members have access to and are responsible for the other members of society. Non-conformist behavior results in social outcasts that are quickly labeled and permanently removed from the hive.

   j꞉ Economy: The Mateen operate a strong economy and have multiple mining interests in and outside of their own systems. They engage in exotic material trade, manufacturing, and defense/munitions sales with other members of the Galactic Council.

   l꞉ Transgalactic Issues: The Mateen have ongoing issues with a breakaway colony. More recently, the Mateen have experienced conflicts with the Jark Empire and occasionally with Hestos.

c꞉ ꞉ꞏHꞏ (Pisky)

   7꞉ Homeworld: Pr'ioski.

   5꞉ Controlled Territory: none.

   n꞉ Physiology

       i꞉ Average height: 4 feet

       ii꞉ Skin color: pink.

       iii꞉ Communication: nonverbal with limited verbal expressions.

       ii꞉ Outstanding features: This small and unassuming species are often mistaken for children by uninformed travelers. They rarely speak and instead prefer to use non-verbal cues. When they do speak, their language is broken and limited to few expressions. Only the severely studied have mastered any spoken language.

   6꞉ Military and Security: The Pisky are refugees on a galactic scale and rely almost entirely on the Galactic Council and member species to provide for them.

h. People and Society: The Pr'ioski people band together in tribal communities. Resulting natural disasters followed by opportunist groups on Pr'ioski has left their planet uninhabitable and most of the culture and knowledge of the Pisky were abandoned along with their planet. One male mates with multiple females, but relationships between males and females are not exclusive. Many times throughout a year, males and females will have multiple mates.

i. Economy: The Pisky have no economy but dedicate themselves to low skill labor and barter within small communities.

u. Transgalactic Issues: Permanent refugees.

e. ᴜ᷄ᴛᴏ᷄ᴛ᷉ɪʜ᷇ᴛᴜ (Radaishar)

f. Homeworld: Mateen.

g. Controlled Territory: Fringe Space and deep space asteroid colonies.

n. Physiology

    i. Average height: 8 feet.

    ii. Skin color: reddish-gray.

    iii. Communication: verbal.

    iiii. Outstanding features: The Radaishar are an extremist group of Mateen that have removed the part of their brain that allows telepathic communication. Their bodies will look diseased as a result of these surgical interventions.

b. Military and Security: Radaishar have no known military and limited security forces.

h. People and Society: Believed to have been a lost Mateen colony, the Radaishar have quietly flourished in fringe space, an area of space at the very edges of the galaxy. Very little is known about current Radaishar society after their battle for independence in 613 GRE, however, it is believed to be similar to the Mateen.

i. Economy: Unknown, suspected piracy and black-market trade.

- Transgalactic Issues: Ongoing conflict with the Mateen collective. Minor security conflicts between Galactic Council member species as a result of piracy and black-market trade.

ᛝ ᚺᛝᚺᚺᛁᚱᚼ (Tassian)

- Homeworld: Tassi.
- Controlled Territory: N/A.
- Physiology
  - Average height: 5 to 6 feet.
  - Skin color: pale skinned, sometimes described as reflective in sunlight.
  - Communication: verbal.
  - Outstanding features: N/A.
- Military and Security
  - A small fleet is held for planetary defense.
  - Infantry force was reduced to a planetary defense force in favor of corporate galactic security.
  - The Tassians have traditionally relied on a Galactic Council security pact for planetary defense, however, increased nationalism risks a future arms race.
- People and Society: Tassians live in a democratic society where the rule of law is honored. Tassians typically find one mate for life and embrace a small nuclear family. Their society still has remnants of a caste system and upward mobility is difficult without the right connections.
- Economy: Tassi has substantial wealth from tourism because of the continual daylight it receives from its dual-helium suns. While trade has waned recently between Tassi and Hestos, the Tassians still engage in significant trade between the Mateens and various mining colonies.
- Transgalactic Issues: The Tassians endure continued conflicts with the Jark Empire over land disputes.

BEFORE THE JUMP

"I'm telling you, brother, our time has come," the young man whispered, barely able to keep his teeth from chattering.

Draped in the white fur of an animal native to the planet Coridon, the two men huddled together in a hastily built ice cave as the temperature outside plummeted to fifty below zero. They had trained with each other since they were children and were now prepared to graduate together as warriors. All that remained was one final test: survive a week on Mount Horeb. It was simple enough to just survive—the most basic of tasks. But considering that that task meant surviving on a floating mountain in the middle of the Northern Sea during winter, this test became an entirely different story.

"How can you be certain?" his best friend responded, turning his head to look over his shoulder. The two leaned back to back, supporting each other's weight as they shared a tiny white-haired rodent that they had captured in a snare the day before. It was hardly big enough to sustain a child, let alone two grown men, and as Brokk

1

crunched down on the small bones, he knew that the meat wouldn't give him the energy he needed to survive the night.

The Jarks graduated their officers in an unorthodox fashion. While most systems believed that prior to graduation a culmination should be a demonstration of the things one had learned and how they are best applied to interstellar combat, the Jarks believed culmination should be focused inward—on oneself and the qualities that must be honed in order to lead great men into battle.

Brokk thought he agreed, although not entirely at this moment. Teachers had repeatedly drilled tactics into his head for years, and warfare had been the primary subject of debate around the table with his family as well as in class with his peers. He understood warfare, but he had never experienced it.

Surviving on Coridon gave him this opportunity, and in the days he had been there, Brokk had already learned more about himself and what it took to survive than ever before. There would be no help, and many of his brothers over this week would die. But those who survived, those who made it, they were the future, forged on the icy peak of the coldest habitable planet of the galaxy and ready to do battle on behalf of their people.

Brokk's teeth continued to chatter as he tried sucking the marrow out of the rat's leg bone before throwing the very last fragment into his mouth. "Because you and I are going to graduate tomorrow," he managed to sputter out, grinding the bone with his teeth.

"We won't survive the night if we don't get any more food. I can't keep warm," Lago complained.

He was right. They had to go out again. In the face of utter exhaustion and frigid temperatures, calories were essential, and right now, calories were what the two of them lacked. Brokk pushed himself to his feet and offered a hand to his red-skinned friend. "Then let's hunt," he said with a grin, trying to show courage in the face of extreme doubt.

Flame from their candle danced and glistened off the icy walls of their hastily built shelter, and Lago's white teeth shone from behind long strands of gray fur draping off his hood as he returned an eager smile. "I'll lead," he said at last, accepting Brokk's hand and pulling himself to his feet. "Besides, I'm a better tracker than you anyway."

The fierce wind howled as they left their shelter in search of food. Merely stepping out into the cold sucked the breath from their lungs and left the two gasping for frigid air to fill their blood with the oxygen they so desperately craved. Brokk staggered into the snow, trying to catch his breath, and imagined that this must be how it felt to be sucked from a damaged hull into the lifeless void of interstellar space. *Perhaps a bit more terror though.*

One following the other, the two aspiring warriors tilted their bodies away from the wind and attempted to walk perpendicular to it. Facing into the freezing blast would send icy daggers through the openings in their hoods and could permanently damage any exposed skin on their faces in mere seconds. Silently, the two trudged through barren trees, using webbed snowshoes to keep them on the surface. With each step, pain shot through their bodies from lifting fatigued legs. Their arms, heavy and worn, strained as they painstakingly drove ice prods into the ground ahead to ensure that they weren't about to fall through a weak patch of snow and land in a gully. A prod to the left and a step with the left foot. A prod to the right and a step with the right foot. *Prod, crunch, prod, crunch, prod, crunch, prod.* It was slow going, and Brokk's stomach roared with hunger. Finally, Lago turned around to face Brokk.

"I'm lost!" he shouted over the wind. "Which way was the canyon?"

"I think you're right," Brokk responded, motioning forward. Lago shrugged and turned again to continue his movement. The wind wailed as the storm drove snow off nearby peaks and pushed bursts of icy sleet into their faces, but the two pressed onward, further away from their camp and into the coming night.

Lago continued to lead. *Prod, crunch, prod, crunch, prod, crunch, prod.* The rhythm captivated Brokk and took his mind far from icy blasts, painstaking steps, and frozen fingers. In his desperation for comfort and aware of its power, Brokk allowed himself to be mesmerized by it, focusing on nothing but the familiar noise. *Prod, crunch, prod, crunch, prod. Prod, crunch, prod, crunch.* Silence.

Lago was gone. "Lago!" Brokk shouted, running to the spot he had last seen him. "Lago!" he bellowed again, fearful that the wind blew his voice back into his throat rather than outward toward his companion. Through the wind and snow, he approached a small ledge; Lago lay twenty feet below, unmoving. "Lago!" he shouted again from his hands and knees, careful not to lean too far over the small pit that had opened up from the weight of their steps.

Lago twitched his mitt-covered hand and groaned. "I think I broke my leg!" he finally shouted.

Brokk could see the snow beneath him turn a reddish hue as it absorbed blood from his now-exposed wound. *Broken...and maybe worse.* But beyond the blood-stained snow was a far more terrifying sight. On the other side of his narrow ridge, a dense nitrogen-composed fog began to climb up from the valley below. At a frigid minus three hundred and twenty degrees, the gas would not simply freeze Lago; it would make him feel as if he were on fire while turning the blood in his veins into solid ice.

"I'm coming down there for you," Brokk shouted back, grabbing at the climber's rope he had looped over his shoulder and searching for a nearby anchor point.

"We'll both die," Lago screamed. "Don't!"

It was too late. Brokk was a man of action and had already secured the rope to a tree and tossed the remainder down to the gorge below. Rappelling to the bottom, he rushed to disconnect his rope and deploy the emergency avalanche shelter he kept in his backpack. The gas had reached the ridge now, and icy fingers stretched out from the fog, begging Brokk to let it feast on their exposed skin. Finally at Lago's side, Brokk gripped his shoulders and pulled him into the small shelter, which was barley large enough for one man. "I guess we'll both die then," he muttered into Lago's ear, zipping the tent behind them.

CHAPTER ONE

Brokk stared intently at the red-streaked sky as beads of sweat rolled off of his golden skin. The eight-foot tall, broad-shouldered behemoth was large, even for Jarkian standards, but he was a half-breed, and mixes between Tassis and Jarks were known to be some of the most formidable warriors in the galaxy. In part, this is why the Jarks were able to live a relatively peaceful existence—there were few people who cared to challenge them and even fewer who lived to brag about a victory against the massive creatures.

Unfortunately, there was another reason the Jarks remained largely unchallenged in their corner of the galaxy. All the planets in their solar system were oversized and orbited either too close or too far from their star. While two of their planets remained in the habitable zone, they just barely did so. The Jark home world, and the one that Brokk currently resided on, was a wretchedly hot planet with an immensely dense core. Its sheer size exerted such gravity on the creatures that were unfortunate enough to live on this planet that their appearances were significantly different compared to more fortunate life elsewhere in the galaxy.

Their second planet, Coridon, rested just within the habitable zone on the other side. While Jark rarely dropped below one hundred and twenty degrees Fahrenheit, Coridon was a winter wonderland that never rose above thirty degrees Fahrenheit. The two twin planets, enormous in size and barely habitable, had masked the Jarkian existence for millennia and allowed them to develop into the race they were today with minimal interference. When the Jarks finally did announce themselves to the other races throughout the galaxy, a galactic order had been established and few cared to break galactic law and challenge the new race.

This peace, however, didn't prevent the Jarks themselves from seeking something greater. For centuries, Brokk and his forefathers had been taught about a great injustice that was dealt their ancestors by the hands of the Tassi. They knew there was a solar system that was rightfully theirs, a solar system that they had been cheated from, and one that would make life easy for all Jarks if they could get it back. Even though Brokk had never seen a picture of Tassi, he felt it calling to him. Returning to Tassi was his destiny.

Brokk stared intently at the sky because tonight, this very night, he was to command a legion of starships to attack the Tassi system. He had studied for years and understood Tassi tactics. Scouts had already been dispatched and reported the size and location of Tassian defenses, and Jark artillery was prepared to fire interstellar munitions at his command. Most important of all, the loosely affiliated galactic order was too incompetent to halt their unannounced advance. By the end of the month, the Tassian system would belong to the Jarks and Brokk would become their chancellor.

"Dreaming about Tassi?" Lago shouted with a smile from behind, ripping Brokk from his reverie. The two had grown up together, fought together, and were now reaching for the prized system together. There was only one final matter to attend to: a sacrifice to the dead in exchange for a blessing on their campaign. This was a tradition that dated back far beyond Brokk's ancestors, and a tradition that he would certainly not forsake.

Lago was pure Jark and was significantly stouter than the golden-skinned half-breed. His skin was reddish bronze was covered in a swirl of curly dark hair. He stooped slightly, preferring to rest his thick arms on the ground to support his large torso. While the Jarks often walked upright, the thick atmosphere and weighty gravity caused them to develop a preference for resting on all fours.

Despite his beast-like appearance, Lago was a brilliant mind who was devoted to the study of applying astrophysics toward military tactics. The two of them were inseparable and, despite having no blood connection, were closer than brothers could ever hope to be. At Lago's approach, Brokk brightened, and any fear or doubt he had about the mission before them suddenly dissipated.

Brokk, whose Tassian genetics insisted that he remain standing upright, spun around to greet him. "Lago! I had hoped you'd come find me!" he responded, smiling and opening his arms for a warm greeting.

The two embraced each other and separated again. "I wouldn't miss it for the world. We've come here together every time before leaving home…you know how much I like the cliffs," Lago responded, shifting his gaze to the city beyond, where buildings as black as night shot upwards from the volcanic landscape.

Brokk knew, and Brokk loved the cliffs himself. The massive rock structure jutted out over the volcanic rock below and provided a spectacular view of both the city and the sea, and no matter which way one turned, the ferocity of the world was captured in an unmistakable majesty. The outcropping's thickness allowed it to hang for hundreds of meters beyond the shore line—and the two men always insisted on stepping out onto the farthest point.

"Did I ever tell you why I come here each time?" Brokk asked.

Lago, now standing upright and shoulder to shoulder with Brokk, shrugged, indicating that he had never thought about it. The star they orbited was a red giant, at the end of its stellar lifespan, and rays imbued with deep reds and oranges constantly bombarded the atmosphere of their massive home world. Red clouds, engorged with a mixture of water and sulfuric acid, stretched across the burned orange sky. *A picturesque night to mark their historic victory.*

"This is why we'll win," Brokk answered, giving him a moment to reflect before continuing. "Look at this place. It's awful!" he joked. "There isn't anyone tougher than a Jark."

Lago laughed. "You have to remind yourself that?" he asked, still chuckling.

"It helps," Brokk responded with a grin. Brokk turned his

shoulders and pointed toward the sky to show Lago what he was looking at before he had arrived. Just off the nose of the cliffs to the north, a massive battleship could be seen maneuvering along the skyline. The ship's bronze, dual-pronged nose was unmistakable against its dark gray exterior. It was Brokk's, and it was the head of the armada conducting its final checks before joining the remainder of the fleet in the upper atmosphere. "Are you ready, Brokk?" Lago asked.

Brokk stared at Lago for a moment longer before returning his golden eyes to the horizon. "I've never been more ready in my life, Lago," he insisted. "We're a battle-hardened fleet, and with you by my side, we are unstoppable. The promised system will be ours again." Brokk looked down at his red-and-black battle uniform. Red was reserved for ship and fleet commanders and helped the crew tell them apart in the heat of a battle. On his wrist was a holographic display that could project information anywhere. In battle, he often allowed it to hover data in the corner of his eyes so that he could see everything at once; during planning sessions the device depicted three-dimensional displays to help his commanders visualize the battlefield. Today, he simply used it to tell the time.

"The artillery bombardment should be commencing soon. We'll start getting updates within the hour," Lago responded.

Brokk smiled. Jark artillery was second to none in the known universe. They had developed a weapon that was capable of firing explosives from outside a planetary system by creating temporary shortcuts through space. The Jarks would chose a planet not more than a few light years from their target, establish an artillery platform, and then create temporary wormholes with which to sling rounds onto the planet below. The system was stealthy and dreadfully effective. Best of all, it was nearly immune to a counterattack. An entire planet's computer systems and defenses would be consumed by locating and defeating the source of the barrage while the armada attacked from the opposite side.

"I'm going to reward you when I become Chancellor," Brokk said. "You'll live better than you ever have."

Lago didn't respond and the two turned to walk back down the rock face toward the offering below. An infant Jark lay helpless, naked, and screaming on a black stone platform. The hardened volcanic stone rocked gently as it floated in a soupy mercury pool that bled from the planet's interior. Brokk's watch flickered and vibrated on his wrist, indicating that it was time to ask the dead to bless his cause. On cue, six Jark priests, robed in gold, stirred the mercury bath beneath the child. As they stirred, they hummed in monotonous unison.

The words they sang were unknown to all but the six who sung them. This was the language of the dead, and as they stirred the mercury it began to boil, reflecting the deep red streaks from the sky above. The silver soup bubbled and popped, the baby rocked violently back and forth, and the priests suddenly erupted in loud chanting, inviting their dead—the souls of billions—to accept this innocent sacrifice and give them the military victory they required.

Hands now appeared—filthy, hair-covered hands, coated in the slime of the mercury and taking on the colors of the sky above. Brokk counted one at first, but like the heads of a hydra, the hands slithered and grabbed at the rock, desperate for the crying infant bathed in the warmth of the life that he possessed. Suddenly, the rock flipped, the hands disappeared, and the humming stopped. Their ritual was over. The dead had accepted Brokk's sacrifice; he would achieve the victory he desired.

Silently, the six priests and two commanders descended from their rocks to their city below. "I think I'll miss this city," Lago finally said.

"We'll build an even greater one on Tassi," Brokk boasted.

CHAPTER TWO

Rays of sun beat down hard against Casika's face as she lay on a fine white sand beach overlooking the bay. It was hot. *Too hot.* Beads of sweat accumulated on her forehead and neck and tickled her skin as they rolled down the cracks and crevices of her body, eventually finding escape into the sandy ground below.

Casika was facing the crystal blue water, but she wasn't watching it. Her throat, as dry as the sand beneath her body, ached and burned, crying out for a drop of liquid. *How long had it been since her last drink? Too long.* Red and blue kites fluttered in the wind, scurrying to and fro on invisible currents as beach goers came to celebrate the day of a united Tassi. A holy day in their beautiful city that was marked with joy for most and sadness for Casika. *United,* Casika scoffed, *maybe for the rich. Maybe for the haves, but not for all of us.*

The crowd angered her; rich people coming from other planets to take advantage of the poor. Rich people eager to buy and sell and drink and sleep while people on Tassi suffered. *Not all people, Casika, just you.*

Just me, she considered.

A shadow moved from the corner of her eye. A middle aged man, sweaty from the same dual suns that perpetually scorched their planet and heading into the water for a dip. *Time to strike.* Casika grinned. She couldn't contain herself, watching his shirtless torso and bare feet prance through the hot sand that burned his feet until he reached the water.

She rolled and pushed herself to her knees, reaching out to her left and securing the cool sparkling drink. The cold bottle was moist with dew from the scorching temperatures outside and in a moment of pleasure she pulled it to her neck and closed her eyes, letting the dew mingle with her sweat and cool her body.

Red liquid fizzed and bubbled as she twisted the top. Her mouth salivated. Dew jumped from the bottle and splashed her lips as she pressed them to the opening. Tilting her head back, alcohol infused water burned against her tongue and throat as she chugged the carbonated treat.

"Hey!" came a man's voice from below. *Caught in the act by some rich clown that's too cheap to just let it go.* Casika opened her throat wider to gulp as he charged up the hill, angry and ready to ask her why she had the nerve to steal his drink. He stopped suddenly, halfway between the sea and the thief. A shadow in a cloudless sky formed above her. Suddenly aware that the man was not alone, Casika saw others on the beach gasp and point. Kites, released from their sailors' grip, fluttered upward into the currents and disappeared.

Satisfied, Casika dropped the bottle from her lips and turned. A black circle had formed in the sky and small white steaks flowed from it. "What is that?" she heard herself say. No answer; even the appalled man remained silent.

More blackness appeared, ovals and circles suddenly formed in the sky; opening from nothing. White dots appeared in the blackness beyond as if Casika was given a window to the stars through a telescope. But there was no telescope, and staring at the stars in the middle of the day was *impossible. Shouldn't be.*

The blackness grew and darkness engulfed the sky and the beach below. What started off as a blackness above continued with a rumble, sand shaking below her knees and powerful enough to rattle her teeth. Noise followed, bursts as loud as thunder shook and in the blackness darker than the night of the dual sunned planet, flashes of white light erupted from the city center.

Think, Casi, think, she told herself, looking at the sky again which seemed to be ripping and tearing from some invisible force beyond the planet and darkness, as black as space itself, threw the white objects onto the city below.

Time to go. Don't need to watch any longer. Get out. Get home. In seconds Casika collected her stuff, which consisted of a glass bottle half full of red liquid she decided she might need later and sprinted towards the road that lined the waterfront. *What home?* She suddenly realized.

Once on the road she dashed between cars that had suddenly filled the streets. The rumbles increased as the darkness engulfed the sky, flickering in and out as the black circles opened and closed. White objects with tails like comets fell gracefully, but with each streak came another violent shudder. *Earthquake? No.* Her mind raced from question to answer, desperate to determine the cause, eager to find the safest place to go. *Meteor shower? What meteor opens the sky?* She countered. In her heart, Casika already knew the answer.

Attack, her mind screamed as she raced towards the city, stopping in her tracks as she realized she was heading the wrong direction. On cue, confirming her assumptions, other explosions burst up from the ground. Cannon fire. Counter fire. *Attack,* her mind screamed again.

The ground shuttered, this time so violently that she fumbled her drink and dropped it to the ground, sending glass and red liquid shattering into her bare legs and staining her white shorts. *No time, klutz,* she ordered. Get out. *Attack,* she screamed again. This time her body got the hint and her legs took off with nowhere to go. *Out, Casika, that's where.*

No home to go to was freeing; no property to save. Vagrancy across the city planet was simple enough to abandon when things got serious. *Things just got serious.*

Suddenly the surface-to-air cannons went silent, confirming her theory that she was now running in the right direction. *Had they hit the defenses?* Casika looked back as she ran to see fire jumping from building to building. Cars blazed and exploded as others joined her in the foot race. Everything she saw began to catch fire and burn. A once-blue oasis now ablaze with rich red, made even richer by the pure white light pouring down from the helium stars above—but now, instead of glory, they were illuminating a nightmare reserved for the sorrows of a story book rather than for her own reality.

For an event so catastrophic to have been completely unannounced, on their holy day, could mean only one thing—the Tassian government had no idea it was going to be attacked, and it was caught entirely unprepared. *Keep running; get out. Take advantage of the vagrancy and being abandoned by family. Abandon them and don't look back. Where. The port, that's where.*

Exhausted from running, Casika summoned all of her strength to sprint toward the space port. She could already see transport vessels firing their thrusters in a desperate attempt to clear the planet's atmosphere. Dodging in and out of pedestrians who were fleeing in all different directions, clueless about where to go or what to do. This shouldn't be happening. *Not here. Not ever. The port, the vessels. So close*, she allowed hope to propel her further.

One hundred meters. She arrived now and could see the gates. Tourists pushed and shoved to get through, but they had families and had to stay together; she was alone, her one advantage. Squeezing through the crowd, she could see the ships, hundreds of them on the flight line loading up passengers and firing engines.

Fifty meters, maybe less. The faster she ran the more desperate she became, worried that her legs might betray her and no longer drive her forward. Her side ached and her heart pounded. Her lungs throbbed under the weight of the fear-induced adrenaline that surged through her organs and inspired her body to press onward.

It was then that she noticed it; a hole appear in the sky just above the spaceport and a single white line fall from the heavens to her planet below. A distinct whistle could be heard, one that she had never heard before, yet suddenly she knew exactly what it was that had been bombarding their world. *Artillery*. This was an artillery barrage similar to stories that only the old would tell around the dinner table. A barrage that she had only learned about in school and seen in the movies, before the times of peace and order. *Artillery*. And with the barrage came the dreadful truth that this was not just an attack, it was an invasion.

As she ran toward the ships, her mind told her to turn around and run the other way, but she couldn't. Her legs wouldn't allow it. She watched, frozen in the moment as the bomb fell towards the airfield; towards Casika. It was as if time itself had slowed to a creep and her whole purpose for living was to be absorbed in this moment. She saw its silver color, its oval shape, and its sharp fins. She saw it all, but she couldn't stop herself from running toward it. Propelled by the same hope that brought her to the port and towards the ships; towards safety. *A mirage.*

The black tarmac sunk down like gelatin upon impact, and a visible wave of pressure erupted out of the black asphalt and upward toward the sky. In violent response, the tarmac, containing hundreds of transport ships exploded outward, like a bed sheet being fluffed, and then it splintered into a thousand pieces. Suddenly, an immense weight from the force of the explosion surrounded and pushed against Casika, accompanied by a white light. Her ears popped, and her eyes bulged as if a suction cup was attempting to extract her brain through any opening it could find. It was excruciating, and she screamed and yelled, but then, she was weightless, and her very existence felt oddly at peace until everything went black.

CHAPTER THREE

By the time Brokk reached the bridge of his battleship, the artillery bombardment was in its final stages. Scouts tasked with reporting the locations for his artillery to attack reported mixed success against the planet's main defenses. On the large viewing screen, a map of the solar system was displayed, highlighting planetary and lunar defenses that were still active, as well as which units Brokk's staff had assigned to ensure the destruction of those defenses. As Brokk suspected, as soon as the bombardment commenced, the Tassian planet swarmed with fighters and battleships searching desperately for the source of their attackers.

As the solar system filled with warships on both sides, reports of skirmishes surged into his battle officer's computers, and as they did, his staff populated those reports into the galactic battle map as soon as they could be analyzed. To Brokk, it appeared as if the Tassi had been successful in deploying some of its fleet, but the majority of the Tassian starships were destroyed on the airfields during the initial artillery barrage. How many starships remained in the fleet was extremely important to Brokk, and the precise reporting on the destruction of enemy battleships was essential to his timeline for committing the remainder of his fleet. Brokk couldn't allow for a Tassian destroyer to catch them off guard from behind a moon and inflict any casualties that would otherwise be easily avoided. Until he knew exactly who and what remained, Brokk was nervously pacing through the operations center, examining maps and reports, and overseeing the progress of the battle.

Without time on their side and a necessity to keep momentum in his favor, Brokk looked to his battle officer and ordered the deployment of the first battle group. The first Jark battle group consisted of three destroyers and a Juggernaut-class battleship that was capable of deploying hundreds of maneuverable space fighters to engage and confuse enemy spaceships. In space, where life and death was merely a mathematical formula between time, distance, and the number of entities on the battlefield, Brokk would take all of the fighters he could muster.

The Juggernaut itself was the crown jewel of the Jark fleet, and Brokk especially liked its name. Deep in Jarkian history, a Juggernaut had been a wagon bearing a picture of the Jarkian god, rolling over the heads of willing devotees. Brokk thought it more than appropriate for his battleship to be the representative of such a bloody lineage and hoped he could contribute to that lore through his actions today. While Brokk's fleet was composed of primarily offensive weapons, he also had a dozen transport ships to carry the first iteration of ground troops to the planet below.

As soon as the order to deploy was given, the main display in the command center switched from the battle map to an image off the left side of the vessel. Three lasers fired alternating bursts of energy into the space in front of the battle group, causing the stars within the target area to begin to wave and flutter as if being viewed through water. After a moment, the stars disappeared, entirely replaced by a bright white light intermingled with red and blue. They had opened a wormhole directly into the Tassian solar system and would arrive in a matter of minutes.

While wormhole travel required a substantial amount of energy, each destroyer was equipped with the ability to open and sustain wormholes as the vessels travelled through. As advanced as its travel was, each ship was still required to open its own tunnel through space because the volatility of wormhole travel refused to allow ships to occupy the same tunnel safely. Soon, the entire battle group had fired its lasers and simply disappeared from view. Once the travel had been completed, Brokk switched his viewing screen back to the battle map and began ordering his ships to clear the outer planets.

The Tassian home world was one of the most unique in the galaxy. There were five planets that orbited two suns, each with their own moons. The home world itself was massive and rested in between the suns. The home world was so large that it occupied nearly the entire habitable zone of the first sun. The second sun, about half the size of the first, sandwiched the home world between the first as it too orbited the first sun. Beyond those two stars were four other planets, one of which was habitable. The entire system was also surrounded by an asteroid belt.

The uniqueness of the dual-sun system made it very difficult to determine where enemy ships could be hiding, partly because of the immense amount of radioactive and magnetic energy pouring from each sun, but also because the moons orbited in oblong patterns that stretched his offensive force to the max. As a result, Brokk could not simply scan for enemy ships from a safe distance; his fleet had to physically observe areas in order to clear them, thus dividing his forces while making them vulnerable to attack. While all of this took time, Brokk was confident that he could keep the pressure on the planet's defense forces, using artillery to ensure that the inhabitants had no chance to pause and consider their options.

As the battle group exited the wormhole in the Tassian system, reports to Brokk's computer began pouring in. The battleship, safely nestled in the center of the battle group, launched its fighters to begin sweeps of the most distant moons, working inward. As the Jarks patrolled for enemy vessels, they dropped satellite beacons that scanned for and reported activity. Their end goal was to completely envelop the Tassian home world, decimate the Tassian Defense Force, and isolate the planet from the rest of the galaxy.

"How long have the guns been firing?" Brokk asked his fire support officer stationed at a terminal along the right side of the bridge.

"Just over two hours now, sir," the man replied. He wore a blue-and-black flight suit, which distinguished him as a lower-ranking officer on the ship.

"Move them," Brokk demanded. "We can't let them become exposed and fall victim to a counter attack." He paused and waited for the officer to input something into his terminal. "How long until we are up again?"

"They'll be in their secondary firing position in half an hour, sir." The young man responded.

"Good. Keep me updated," Brokk responded. Moving his artillery from one location to the next was essential to keeping their enemy off guard. Brokk knew that while they defended their cannons with a destroyer and multiple fighters, the Tassians' first response would be to obliterate the artillery. Only this would give the Tassians a chance to consolidate their forces for battle against the Jark main fleet. Brokk would not allow that to happen.

Returning his attention to the large screen in front of him, Brokk observed enemy vessels beginning to appear on the far side of the third planet. At first, just one ship was reported by the beacon, but soon there were almost a dozen smaller ships. Worse yet, the Jark scout ship's icon disappeared, indicating that it was destroyed during a skirmish. Two more scouts vanished from his digital map almost as quickly as the first.

"What's going on there?" Brokk demanded over his ship's communications system. He spun the battle map on his wrist to pinpoint the location to his staff in the command center.

"Lago's destroyer is reporting enemy warships, sir," the battle officer responded, turning briefly toward Brokk before getting back onto his terminal to focus on the new battle.

"I need more detail than that!" Brokk ordered. "How many? What type? Are they presently under fire? What are Lago's actions?" Brokk had to know everything—every last detail. The way they fought and won this war would directly affect his ability to control the planet after the battle was over.

"It looks like five Tassian destroyers and a horde of fighters." The battle captain switched the view on the screen to show a beacon's perspective of the developing battle. The Tassian destroyers were massive two-thousand meter long objects flying in an arrowhead formation. The formation allowed them to maximize their frontal fire against Lago's battle group. Already, thousands of lights flashed as the opposing sides exchanged volley after volley of energy rounds and counter-fire measures.

Outmatched. Outgunned. Fighters vanishing in the skirmish as soon as they are launched from the carrier bays. *How long can they last? Should I wait to see if Lago gets the upper hand?* So many questions to answer with so little time.

"Take us there now," he demanded of his pilot, refusing to be paralyzed with indecision. Then, jumping onto his own terminal, he circled a spot in space to the flank of the destroyers and on the near side of the planet for them to make their jump. "Jump us there," he said, pointing. "This will mask us against the planet and allow us to attack their flanks. With any luck, it will break up their formation."

His pilot Terre, who was a seasoned veteran and a master at maneuvering the massive battleship, acknowledged and initiated the jump sequence. Simultaneously, the three remaining battleships in the command battle group created their own wormholes and jumped into the skirmish behind their audacious leader. Mere seconds later, the four ships of Brokk's personal armada ripped through the fabric of space and suddenly appeared on the far side of the Tassian formation. As soon as Brook arrived, he began barking orders to his ships to fight the enemy destroyers.

Between Brokk and his enemy, mangled bodies intermingled with debris floated silently past his viewing screen. Brokk was not a religious man, but for the sake of his crew, he muttered, "Rest in peace," and followed that with a hasty maneuver order to his crew. "Full thrust. Make them pay for killing Jarks," he shouted over the intercom.

Brokk had learned that, oftentimes, the difference between victory and defeat was the motivation of the soldiers leading the charge. He would never admit it, but he cared little for the men who had died. Their sacrifice, however, was far more important. It fueled his men, and it made them sharper, faster, more alert; it made them better. That was what Brokk needed, a desire for revenge. Blood for blood. The effect that death can have on the psyche of a young man should never be underestimated.

As Brokk's armada approached, the Tassian battle group appeared disoriented to the new threat off their starboard flank. Some fighters broke from the arrow formation in an attempt to engage with the Jarkian ships but found themselves alone and outnumbered against Brokk's tightly formed assault. As the Tassian destroyers scrambled to react to the appearing of four new battleships, Lago's formation closed the distance, continuing the barrage of star clusters, energy rounds, and lasers. From the other side, Brokk's formation hammered the flank of the enemy with his own bombardment of kinetic energy rounds. One by one, the Tassian destroyers splintered and exploded, fire erupting from the hulls and terrified Tassian crewmembers choking as they were sucked into the icy abyss.

His crew cheered the mayhem, but Brokk was never one to rest on a previous victory. "Lago, sweep the far side of the planet and then push into an orbit around the main planet. I need your damage report," he calmly ordered into his communications system. "Terre, take us to the near side and slingshot us around the moon. I want to make sure we don't get surprised again." Both Lago and Terre acknowledged their orders and the sweep continued.

"We're up on the guns, sir," the fire-support officer shouted over his shoulder.

"Excellent," Brokk responded. "Target landing zones one, two, and three to prepare for the ground invasion."

Brokk's plan was a lightning-fast attack that would mitigate the planetary defenses and put Jark warriors on the ground mere hours after the fighting began. Instead of working from the outer planets inward, jumping ground troops from moon to moon to seize their final objective, Brokk wanted to seize the home world as soon as possible and simply isolate the second planet from receiving vital supplies. What Brokk lost by controlling the moons he believed was gained back by controlling the home world. Brokk hoped that the blockade, coupled with an artillery barrage, would incite the total Tassian surrender of the second planet and any inhabited moons.

Brokk climbed into his large cream-colored commander's chair that was at the rear center of his U-shaped operations room of the battleship. The chair overlooked his staff of Jark officers and enabled him to visually communicate with the other commanders in his fleet. Pressing a button on his armrest, a small hologram of his entire fleet appeared above his lap and hovered, rotating with the same gravity as the solar system they had just jumped into.

Moving his fingers inside the hologram, he selected three large, rectangular ships out of the formation, and instantly the commanders of those vessels appeared as holograms on the floor of the bridge. These were the commanders of the transport vessels that contained a total of forty million planetary warriors who were to become the occupying force on the main planet. While forty million might seem large, it was small a fraction of the force that Brokk had requested from his national defense agency. Thinking again about being nickel and dimed from his politicians infuriated Brokk when he considered a force of forty million compared to the almost three hundred billion occupants of the main planet.

With the holographs of the ship commanders located on the bridge, Brokk went through the plan. He ensured that his artillery officer briefed the transportation commanders his fire support plan and that Lago briefed them on the air support plan. Once this task was complete, Brokk opened the floor to questions. He was neurotic about details and had rehearsed the plan many times with his subordinates. No one had any questions, so he ordered the transports to initiate their jump sequence from the Jark home world to end with their descent to the planet's surface.

Brokk closed the hologram down, but Lago's image remained on the bridge. "Commander Brokk," Lago said submissively. His demeanor had changed in nearly an instant from best friend to subordinate. Sometimes, it hurt Brokk that they couldn't maintain such a close relationship while working, but he also knew the importance of not showing favoritism. Lago's demeanor suggested that he had something important to say, and by reaching out his hand, Brokk grabbed Lago's image and pulled it back into his armrest. There they could have the conversation privately without transmitting the audio across the ship's speakers for the staff to hear.

What's going on, Lago? Brokk thought into the ship's psycho-transmission system, or PTS for short. A conversation on the PTS device was difficult to get used to, but it became one of the most trusted ways Brokk communicated with his commanders and his superiors. The ability to transmit words into another person's head ensured that conversations remained safe, secure, and oddly intimate because, with each word, came the sender's mental visualization of the sentence he or she had produced. Sometimes, those visualizations came soaked in tears or were on fire from rage, but they always provided the receiver the context of an entire array of emotions in an instant.

Lago, pausing for the transfer to Brokk's personal station to be complete, continued. *In the ambush we lost twelve scout vessels and took significant damage to one of our destroyers.* Even though he looked collected, his thoughts dripped with raw emotion and Brokk was able to see the faces of the pilots that Lago had personally known. He resisted but felt Lago's sorrow too. Brokk knew Lago was not done with the transmission, however, as Lago never wasted time with an emotional report. *I circumvented the outer planets with the remaining destroyers, but with our reduced numbers, I'll need help establishing a blockade around the home world and providing effective air support.* Focused on the mission again, Lago's thoughts were dry, cold, and calculated; they no longer stung from the pain that he had felt mere moments earlier.

Brokk could see from his battle display on the bridge that the remainder of Lago's fleet was desperately trying to establish an effective blockade as hundreds of tourist and merchant ships attempted to escape from the planet's atmosphere. *I'll give you command of a destroyer from my fleet. Is there anything else you need?* Brokk conveyed.

Lago didn't, and they terminated the session.

CHAPTER FOUR

Casika woke to find herself squeezed into the metal corner of a transport ship. Her head ached, and her eyes were blurry, throbbing against her skull as she tried to look around. Pressing her deeper into the rough steel hull were two large Tassians standing and leaning above her on each side. They pretended not to notice that she had woken up, and after some effort, she managed to unwedge her arm from underneath theirs to feel her face. Her hand returned blood from her forehead and nose. *What happened to me?* she thought. At first, Casika couldn't remember a thing, but then it suddenly dawned on her that she must have been knocked unconscious from the explosion on the airfield.

"How did I get here?" she asked softly, trying to make sense of the noisy buzzing that vibrated the steal wall behind her. Neither man responded, and Casika suddenly realized that the ship engines were roaring directly beneath them. The small vessel was crammed with people. *They must have taken everyone they could carry*, she thought, looking around at the other faces. Most looked down as they sat on the floor, stood filling the aisles, or leaned against the walls. "Hey!" she shouted at the man who was practically sitting on her.

He didn't hear her or didn't care to. The engines were too loud and the constant hum was wreaking havoc on her mind. "What happened," she shouted again, doing her best to wrestle herself loose from the wall. Suddenly, the ship shuttered and people gasped. Hands and arms flung upward to grab at walls and ceilings or to grip the seats in front of them, but she had nothing to grab, instead feeling herself crushed by the leg of the man standing above her.

The ship lurched again, this time spinning and banking hard to the right. The roar of the engines pummeled her eardrums, but another noise appeared and disappeared intermittently. It was a sound eerily similar to what she had heard on the surface—that of cannon fire.

What's happening! She screamed in her mind again, desperate, and hot, and confused. He head throbbed and the weight of the man and a dozen other people pushing against her was too much. Her stomach lurched and churned and ached as the small ship banked and rolled.

Hammering outside got louder, tearing into her eardrums and piercing her mind like a screw through wood. *Hey*, she wanted to shout again, desperate for someone to pay her attention and give her room to breathe but as she opened her mouth she felt a surge of saliva and acid trap her words in her throat and threaten to throw her lunch on the man to her front. *Keep your dignity, Casi,* she implored herself. *Hold on a little longer. It's not so bad.*

The hammering of cannons outside and the rocking of the ship told her otherwise. *Ignore it; it's going to be fine.*

***

Trying to seal off the planet from escape was difficult work from space, a truly three dimensional battlefield, but the third destroyer added to Lago's battle group made that task much easier. As soon as the destroyer took its spot on the northern pole of the planet's rotation, it found itself engaged by local planetary fighters defending fleeing transport vessels. Lago's instructions to the destroyer were simple: *Our blockade will not be feared if we allow a single ship to escape. Destroy them all, and the planet will cease sending them.*

With the majority of the sensor beacons deployed around the planet, Lago was able to visually track the details of every little skirmish. While many of the battles didn't last long, Lago found himself transfixed on one transport ship in particular that had suddenly become the focus of enemy escort ships and their own fighters. Try as the fighters might, the enemy escorts were hindering their ships from destroying the tiny vessel. Every time it looked like it would meet its end, the small transporter would bank and roll to avoid the tiny window a fighter had to destroy it before being swarmed again by enemy fighters. If they didn't act fast, it would be beyond the planet's magnetic field and capable of initiating wormhole travel.

"Stop that ship!" Lago shouted to his commanders across the intercom. "It's starting its jump, stop it!" he shouted again. As the escaping ship fired its lasers into space to create the wormhole, one of the Jark fighters fired two heat-seeking torpedoes. Just before the missiles could hit their mark, the ship jumped into the wormhole with the two torpedoes racing through the same portal. "Cross your fingers," Lago said bitterly as he returned his focus to other parts of the blockade.

***

The jump through the wormhole came as a jolt to Casika as she sat on the floor, but it was still a smoother motion than she always imagined it would be. The ship didn't stretch or vibrate as she thought it would. Instead, it felt the way a person does when they let go of the handrails while coming out of a pool, slipping deep into the cool water as the tug of gravity envelops the body. The pressure around her ears abated almost as soon as it started, and before long she felt as if the ship hadn't made the jump into a wormhole at all. *Safe at last*, she allowed herself to think. She thought too soon.

Without her knowledge, two torpedoes fired from a Jark fighter entered the wormhole that the transport vessel had opened and raced to catch up to the fleeing ship with space itself collapsing back into the tunnel that the small ship bore through. The impact of the first torpedo slamming into the left engine knocked Casika's head against a rough steel wall and ripped the small ship sideways, tearing it out of the wormhole. Smashing into the side of the pilot's cockpit mere seconds after the first, the second torpedo rocked Casika's body back and forth against the bulkheads and sent standing passengers flying through cabin.

Flames engulfed the passenger cabin and were only held at bay by the racing of oxygen from the vessel's torn hull. Casika fought for consciousness as the ship spiraled downward toward a small planet below. Fully caught in the planet's gravity, the ship twirled through the thin atmosphere, and a rapidly decreasing amount of air raced from the gaping holes in the small craft as they spun uncontrollably downward.

Terrified passengers grabbed and clung to whatever they could hold onto as the transporter spun wildly out of control. In the chaos, Casika felt someone grab her thigh, but as she reached down to grasp their hand, the person lost his grip and slammed into a far wall before being sucked into the atmosphere beyond. The ship spun and twisted, plastering her head into the wall behind her.

Like a bug caught in a blender, her body was twisted and contorted, smashed and thrown as the planet's gravity seized control of the small ship helplessly falling from the sky. Finally, just as Casika felt she couldn't survive a moment longer, a set of blast doors dropped downward from their compartments, sealing the passenger cabin from the cockpit and repressurizing what was left of the ship's hull.

Before a thought had the chance to enter her mind, the ship's spinning stabilized and jolted to a stop, sending Casika's exhausted body into the ceiling and dropping her back onto the steel platform below. Dizzy, she pushed herself to her knees and tenderly climbed to her feet, using a chair for support. Looking around the cabin, she realized how devastating the blast had been. Of the several hundred people crammed into the ship, she counted only ten remaining. The others must have been pulled into space before the hull had sealed. Of those ten, only four, including herself, seemed to be moving.

Light beamed through a window and Casika's curiosity drove her to it. Stumbling at first, she staggered toward the small circular porthole and looked out to find herself suspended hundreds of feet above the ground. The ship had crashed halfway into a massive alien forest and was now perched atop giant tree limbs and vines, hundreds of feet above the surface. Taking a step back from the window, she found a corner and vomited.

CHAPTER FIVE

Gemini was hiking through the vast Rodamian forest when he saw a small craft plummet through the atmosphere and crash into the trees that lined Farrig's summit, one of three mountain peaks along the southern ridge of the Rodamian mountain range. Rodam was a small, densely forested moon that orbited his home planet, the fifth planet from their yellow sun. Once a year, Gemini would travel to Rodam to spend a few moon orbits hiking along the ridge and visiting old friends who had been buried on the lush moon long ago.

For Gemini, the hikes were a therapeutic reminder that, for even the greatest warriors, life was often fleeting and all too frequently ended prematurely. This wasn't the only reason he went, though. The Mateen were a race of mentalists who had the ability to communicate telepathically to one another. While this ability had been replicated by other races in the galaxy, none were capable of doing this naturally. In fact the galactic order initially categorized the Mateen as having a hive style of communication rather than relying on audible communication.

The Mateen could do both, but preferred to let the order figure that out on its own.

Gemini took these trips for his entire fleet so that its fallen comrades would not be forgotten. He also made sure he could communicate to the men who served under him the pain that he felt on their behalf and the heartache endured as a result of someone's death. The members of Gemini's fleet were lost but never forgotten, and that brought all his warriors great comfort.

For Gemini, this was a holy endeavor that required endurance, courage, and fortitude. The working vacation was also a welcome escape from his busy life in the fleet, where interdicting galactic smugglers, turning away refugees, and maintaining defensive checkpoints had become an exhausting endeavor for the unchallenged space fleet in an era of galactic security.

Gemini wiped the sweat off his coarse gray forehead and counted the seconds from when he saw the craft disappear to when he would hear the impact. This gave him a rough idea of the distance he would have to travel to investigate the crash. After counting to ten, he had heard nothing. *Must have been caught in the trees, Castor,* Gemini reported to his executive officer, using nothing but his thoughts.

Castor was his trusty second hand, who took control of the fleet if Gemini was unavailable. He was a veteran pilot and an excellent soldier, so much so that Gemini trusted Castor with his very life. Moments before the shuttle came through the atmosphere, he had been alerted telepathically by Castor that an unidentified vessel had dropped out of a wormhole near their moon and was on a crash course for Rodam. After several failed attempts at hailing the vessel, they asked Gemini to inspect the crash site. *This had better not be a trap, Castor,* was his response. I'll *climb up for a closer look. See if you can pinpoint its location and send it to me.*

The Mateens were a sturdy people who had enjoyed peace and prosperity in their corner of the galaxy. While their home planet orbited a comparatively cool yellow sun, they earned their ash-like complexion from an interaction between their natural pigment and yeast-like bacteria that all Mateens were exposed to at birth. The result was a rugged-looking people who appeared to have been born out of the mouth of a volcano rather than from nurturing mothers.

In addition to their color, they were a group known for their large stature. A fully grown Mateen man walked on two legs and stood about eight feet above the ground. Large legs supported their powerful torsos, and their history was full of hard, communal work as opposed to conflict and war.

When the Mateens had learned that they weren't alone in the universe, they were stunned that each race had a rocky history full of atrocities against their own people as opposed to community, cooperation, and peace. Gemini determined in his own mind that it was the Mateen ability to communicate telepathically that prevented such bloodshed in the civilization's early history. Simply put, it was far more difficult to slaughter a man when one could personally experience his pain in death. While other races spoke of empathy, Gemini and his people lived it.

This peaceful history and supernatural ability, however, didn't prevent the Mateens from quickly developing a robust military force. Their experience with other races taught them a valuable lesson. Not everyone could collectively experience joy and heartache, and even fewer cared. The other races had inflicted such pain on one another that the Mateens decided that they must never fall victim to the violence of another race, and as one collective, they built one of the largest space fleets in the galaxy.

A largely introverted race that remained isolated in its own solar system, the Mateens were prosperous and caring, and in an effort to make the lives better of the less fortunate, they often received refugees from other planets and did their best to accommodate those in need. With his crew orbiting overhead, Gemini collectively wondered what the circumstances of this vessel were and if it was an omen of things to come or simply the bad luck of a pilot and his crew.

His legs suffering from the thinner atmosphere on Rodam, Gemini climbed the last section of ridgeline that separated him from the crash. He could smell the smoke from smoldering thrusters and could hear the sputtering of damaged engines. Approaching the crash, Gemini saw broken branches above and fluids draining from the ship's interior soaking into the soil below his feet. Mostly water and liquid methane, these fluids were inserted between the ship's dual layer hull to prevent gamma radiation from penetrating to the passenger compartments. Despite corporate claims that this fluid was harmless, Gemini was convinced that exposure would lead to some sort of unique cancer later in life.

Looking up, he finally spotted part of a blue-and-white striped tourist transport vessel suspended between vines and tree branches about fifty feet above the surface. *I guess I get to climb as part of my adventure,* he thought to his executive officer, who responded with a chuckle and an apology. *Prepare a recovery vessel and send it to the surface. I doubt there are any survivors at this point.* His bridge acknowledged, and Gemini once again blocked out the always-present mental chatter from the remainder of his crew. While he could feel the eyes of hundreds of Mateen onlookers in the back of his mind, Mateens learned early in life how to control the intrusion, gain privacy, and enjoy the company of the ever-present collective.

Gemini removed a backpack he had been carrying and fitted his hands and feet with a set of climbing spikes. This would help him grip the tree, but without a rope and only minimal first aid supplies, Gemini had asked his crew to send him a speed bag full of emergency equipment. The bag would be fired from a torpedo bay, slowly drift toward his location once it entered the moon's atmosphere, and should land within a few meters of his location. As he waited, he would climb. Digging his cleats into the thick orange and green barked tree, Gemini began his ascent.

***

Recovered from her sudden sickness, Casika began checking the other people on the ship. The first person she checked wasn't moving any longer. From the stomach down, his waist and legs appeared to have been crushed under a structural support beam in the crash. Casika kneeled down and put her ear near his mouth. He wasn't breathing. His eyes were frozen. She had never seen or even touched a dead body before, and now she found herself surrounded by them.

A pit formed in her stomach, and suddenly Casika felt the urge to vomit again. *Get a grip,* she told herself trying to hold it in. Looking away she decided to move toward the front of the compartment where she had seen and heard two people groaning moments before. Only one was still moving, and her breathing was shallow. It was a light-skinned Tassian female wearing sleek silver pants and a blue blouse.

Once Casika saw her, she rushed over and kneeled down next to her head. The woman opened her mouth to speak, but couldn't; instead, a small amount of blood gurgled up from her throat and coated her lips, pooling in the corners of her mouth before running down her chin and onto the floor. Her face was pale, and Casika had to look away but still searched for and then grabbed the woman's hand.

"Please don't die," Casika begged the woman, beginning to cry. "Please don't die. You can make it. I know you can, you can make it." She paused to look at the woman. Bright blue eyes stared back at her, and fear painted the woman's face with beads of sweat on her cheeks and forehead. "Don't leave me here alone," Casika continued. "It's you and me now, we can make it—I know we can."

The woman blinked and then relaxed her grip in Casika's hand. More blood pooled in her mouth and flowed steadily down her cheek and onto the floor. Casika closed her eyes and wept. She was all alone now.

Suddenly, pounding came from the outside of the ship. "Is anyone in there?" shouted a voice processed and translated by a universal translator implanted at birth behind Casika's ear. "Hello!" It shouted again. The voice was deep and masculine, but it was also short and out of breath.

Casika jumped to her feet and stumbled toward the airlock that the pounding came from. "Hey!" she shouted back, slapping her palms against the inside of the airlock. "I'm here! Please help me!"

"Who else is in there?" the voice asked. "How many are injured?"

"It's just me," Casika responded. The impact of her saying it out loud was like a hammer slamming into her chest. *Just me, of hundreds, just me.*

"Are you hurt?" it asked again. "Can you unlock the door? I need you to help me get in."

Casika found a yellow emergency latch that lay horizontal across the large door. Using as much strength as she could muster, she depressed the latch and pushed downward.

Two bolts shrieked and popped angry as Casika separated them against their will as the lock disengaged from the door. It hissed, and the rescuer pulled the door open from the outside.

In the smoke from airlock, all Casika could see at first was a shadow. But as his face appeared, Casika threw herself backward and scrambled for the far wall. "Please don't hurt me!" she spontaneously cried out when she saw him.

Entering the craft was a massive man with crimson red eyes and a face that was as gray as stone. Deep lines carved across his forehead and down his cheeks. His neck was thick and his torso huge. The man towered over the door for a few seconds while he looked around through the cabin. Instead of approaching her, he kneeled down and put his stony gray hands on the woman who had just died. He paused for a minute and then approached the trembling Casika.

Casika squeezed as far as she could against the wall. She had never seen anyone like this man. As he reached out, she squirmed, but when he touched her forehead, she found herself instantly comforted. Despite the rocky appearance of the man's skin, his hands were warm and soft. His crimson eyes penetrated deep into hers from behind his dark gray brow, but not as evil or malicious; there was a kindness that hid behind the color, a kindness that penetrated as deep as his soul.

"You look OK; maybe a concussion. How do you feel?" he asked, his voice thundering off the metallic walls as he spoke. "Are you nauseas?"

Nauseas? What a dumb question. Didn't he feel nauseated in here too? Casika relaxed her body a bit. Forgetting the question, and instead finding herself completely transfixed by his gaze. "My head hurts," she murmured. "And my arm."

"It looks like you hit your head pretty hard," he responded, looking at her arm now. "It's a miracle you survived." He paused as he looked around the cabin and then back to Casika. He didn't say anything about the ship, but she knew what he thought. It was a soup can. A blender. She should be dead. "Before I take you off this shuttle," he continued, "I need to know why you crashed on one of our moons."

"I wish I knew," she responded, looking down at the floor now. "Our planet was attacked; I escaped in this transport vessel. I think we were shot down…I'm from Tassi, do you know Tassi?"

He nodded and paused for a moment. In the instant that he paused, she saw his eyes flicker, not much, but just enough, almost as if they changed color very briefly from a crimson red to a regal gold and back again. Rising to stand, the man reached out his arm as an offer to pull her to her feet. "I'm Gemini, and I hope you aren't afraid of heights because it's a long climb down."

CHAPTER SIX

Wormhole travel was a relatively new form of transport within the galaxy. While most occupied systems had the capability to create and travel through wormholes, none of them to Brokk's knowledge had any ability to observe activity that was occurring within a wormhole. The travel itself was so unstable that while it was being developed, only the bravest ship captains dared to even utilize it as a viable method of traversing the galaxy. The danger came with the function of the wormhole itself. Ships would create folds in space using highly focused beams of exotic energy that was dense enough to literally press space down on itself. As the space was pressed down, it connected two previously untouching areas in a manner similar to folding a sheet, at which point all the ship had to do was step across, repress the space, and take another step. All of this happened extremely fast, and the slightest malfunction could leave one stranded halfway between the starting point and the intended destination.

Worse yet, because it was so difficult to control the direction that the computer decided to step, one might attempt to skip along the top of a black hole only to be sucked into the worst anomaly possible halfway through a journey.

The greatest galactic minds developed what they called "dead zones" in the computer system. These zones attempted to tell the ship where it could and couldn't step over, but even that was deeply rooted in the theoretical. While nearly everyone used wormhole travel, very few cared to admit that they had absolutely no idea if it was going to be their last second alive.

For the sake of the current campaign, Brokk found himself desperately hoping that the volatility of wormhole travel was tipping in the Jarks' favor. Moments ago, Lago had informed him that a transport vessel carrying Tassians had escaped the blockade. This was extremely disturbing to Brokk for a variety of reasons, and he hoped that soon they would have information about where the ship exited the wormhole and if it had been destroyed by the two torpedoes.

The first reason Brokk was angered was that the blockade had to be absolutely impenetrable. If any vessel could escape, the Jarks risked the Galactic Council's intervention in their invasion earlier than planned. The Jarks would be forced to comply with peacekeepers, inspectors, health workers, and a variety of other bureaucratic nonsense that they simply weren't interested in. If, however, the Jarks could establish a ceasefire with the Tassians, gain control of the government, and negotiate with the Galactic Council on their own terms, they stood a much greater chance of absolute victory.

The second reason Brokk was irate was that he knew the ancient writings. Not only was Tassi rightfully the Jarks to take, but the Tassians were to be completely obliterated. Any trace of the Tassian race elsewhere in the galaxy was an insult to the Jarks and their forefathers. The scriptures were absolutely clear that the Tassians not only deserved death but had cheated the Jarks out of everything that was rightfully theirs. They were scum, living on a stolen planet, drinking stolen water, and breathing stolen air, while good, hardworking Jarks suffered on a molten second-rate home land. This, in part, is the reason that they chose to attack the planet on a day all Tassians would travel back to their home world to celebrate their holiday. None could survive.

The Jark blockade and subsequent governing would repay the Tassians for a treachery that was long overdue. In the process, Brokk would become the most famous Jark to have ever lived and would establish an empire that endured forever. As Brokk fumed, Lago's voice erupted over the intercom. "We have a location on the ship and confirmed hits from the torpedoes. It's too early to say, but I don't believe there were any survivors."

"Where's the ship?" Brokk asked coldly, ignoring Lago's intuition and instead demanding facts.

"When the first torpedo struck, the ship was knocked out of the wormhole and into the Mateen system. It crashed on one of their moons. We've tried to—"

Lago was cut off by an incensed Brokk. "The Mateens?" he snarled, leaping from his commander's chair and searching for something to destroy. "It would have been better for them to have stayed in the wormhole!" he fumed. This was the problem with wormholes. It was hard to know where a ship might come out if it exited the tunnel early.

Lago waited for a moment, silent, and then continued where he left off. "We've tried to scan the surface, but their defenses block our more sensitive scanners. We would have to get much closer to their system to get a real look at the situation." He paused again, and after some silence, Lago continued. "Would you like for me to dispatch a destroyer?"

Brokk sat back in his chair and thought. The Mateens were a tough race and most likely couldn't be bullied. They remained isolated because of their disdain for others, not because of their fear of them. While the Jarks had very little interaction with the Mateen, Brokk had studied their tactics back at school and understood them to be extremely formidable. In fact, it was the Mateen telepathic ability that forced the Jarks to develop their own ways of communicating using psycho transmissions. The ability to think and respond as a single entity was an uncanny capability in the realm of space combat.

Luckily for Brokk, the Mateens were also complete isolationists, and even if there were survivors, it was unlikely that they would interact with the Galactic Council. Their distrust for other races in the galaxy might work in Brokk's favor. Still...loose ends had to be tied up and the prophecy fulfilled. Brokk wasn't sure he wanted to entrust such an important task on a destroyer. What message would that send to the Mateens if he insulted their Fleet Captain with a mere ship captain?

"I'll go there myself," Brokk finally replied over the intercom. "Lago, you are in command until I return. Ensure the ground invasion goes as planned, and report any significant events to me. The next stage will take the longest, so let's ensure we resupply our ships and prepare to give our terms to the Tassian government. Don't screw up again, Lago."

Brokk cut off the transmission before Lago could acknowledge his orders and looked toward his veteran pilot. "Terre, take us to the outskirts of their system and hail the Mateen headquarters ship. I want them to know we are coming. Tell them I want to speak to their commander in reference to our pursuit of Tassian revolutionaries that are wanted in connection with a plot against our home world."

Terre acknowledged his commander and initiated the jump sequence. *Even the best plans hit a few road bumps,* Brokk thought resentfully.

CHAPTER SEVEN

After treating Casika's wounds using the first aid kit he carried with him, Gemini contacted Castor to determine where they would conduct a linkup and transfer their guest to receive medical attention onboard his ship. Gemini wanted to stay on the surface longer, but intuition told him that he would be needed at his command center in the event that this was more than just a refugee vessel. While wormhole travel was dangerous, it was rare that something simply fell out of the sky. If there was even the possibility that the vessel had been shot down as the young woman suggested, he would be needed on his ship for what might happen next.

Walking through the orange-and-green forest together, Gemini found himself wishing he could use his telepathy to peer into Casika's mind. He had too many questions and doubted the objectivity that her filtered and emotionally raw responses would bring. Unfortunately for him, the effortless mental communication that was enjoyed by all members of the Mateen people was useless on other races. This was an adaptation that required both a sender and a receiver, and so far, only the Mateens met the criteria for both.

Despite the obvious barrier, Gemini still wished there was an easier way to learn the truth, a way that didn't involve the subjectivity of personal testimony. She was a striking-looking female, with long white hair that sparkled like crystals in the sunlight, a welcome change from the large Mateen women with hair so black it absorbed almost any light that dared to saturate it. The way she walked was light and full of vigor despite what had just happened moments ago, but she also thrust her shoulders forward as if she carried a heavy back pack, and her face was wrought with worry.

"I'm sorry for all the people you lost," Gemini said. "Did you know them?"

"No," she replied, continuing to walk forward. "I didn't know any of them. But I'll never forget some of them. I just keep thinking about their faces. I've never seen anyone die before."

Gemini had. He had seen people die more times than he could count. With each death, he felt their fear, he participated in their final thoughts, and he pledged to each one that he would look after their families. Then he buried them, all of them, on this moon. Gemini had endured too much loss, but that was the life he had chosen and his burden was shared among all of his crew. Suddenly, Gemini realized that Casika wasn't the only one who would have trouble applying objectivity to the truth of her experiences. His own bias flared against whomever had shot this vessel down and sent hundreds of lives into the void of space. And then he realized another thing. Without the full story, he had already believed her story—that the ship had been shot down.

"What will you do to me?" she asked anxiously, cutting into his thoughts and tearing him from the past.

"Were you telling the truth?" Gemini asked in a way that inextricably linked her own future to her past. Once she nodded in the affirmative, he continued. "We're going to make you well onboard my ship, then I will notify the Galactic Council of the incident, and then I will send you home."

"There is no home!" she blurted out, spinning around to face him and stopping him in his tracks; engorged tear drops falling from her eyes and rolling down her cheeks. "I'm sorry," she said instantly, dropping her gaze to the ground and cupping her hands together at her mouth. "I'm sorry for…"

Gemini raised his stone-gray hand to silence her, but before he could ask her what she meant, Castor leaped into his mind. *A Jark Battleship just jumped into our system and halted beyond the asteroid belt. Their commander identified himself as Brokk and wants to speak with you. He is tracking fugitives who he believes crashed on Rodam.*

Tell him I am investigating the crash site and will happily meet with him when I return to the ship, Gemini responded, refusing to take his eyes off Casika. "You have a lot of explaining to do once we get on board," he finally told her, reassessing everything he thought he knew about the innocent-looking female.

The two trudged onward in silence the rest of the way to the landing zone. Gemini found himself desperately wishing he could read her mind again and gamed a strategy for determining the truth. As he approached the shuttle, three of his soldiers rushed out to help Casika into the ship and onto a medical bed, while Gemini climbed into the passenger seat and put on a helmet. "Take her to medical and keep her under guard. I'll head to the bridge. Let me know if she says anything," Gemini said over the intercom.

The small white-and-gray shuttle roared, lifting them from the stone outcropping. Tree tops appeared and then faded to dark green and finally disappeared altogether. The rich blue sky became a purple hue and then a black. In the distance, Gemini could see his Battleship. *It'll be good to be home*, he thought.

***

Once on the bridge, Fleet Commander Gemini threw his backpack against a wall, greeted Castor with a warm handshake, and sunk into his chair. His body ached from the hike, and his legs and forearms burned from the climb toward the crashed shuttle. He wasn't as young as he used to be, and this latest experience forced him to admit to himself he needed to carve out more time for exercise. He was glad to be on board his ship to enjoy the comforts that came with being home.

His home was also the crown jewel of the Mateen space fleet. The Shatter Class battleship was the largest and most technologically advanced ship in the entire fleet, and Gemini had twelve of them in his arsenal, along with a variety of destroyers and space carriers. He had divided his fleet into four identical battle groups that were capable of operating independently across the galaxy. Each group contained three Shatter Class battleships, four equinox class destroyers, a carrier, and a variety of sensor and scout ships. Gemini's entire fleet, one of five Mateen space fleets, consisted of over twenty commanders and hundreds of pilots. The Shatter Class, however, was the best of them all, and any man who sat in the commander's seat couldn't help but feel a surge of authority and importance that came with the position.

"So what have we got?" Gemini asked, looking around at the crew running his bridge. The bridge was his ship's command center, and unlike some vessels that placed their command center in the front, his was nestled safely in the interior of the ship. This made it extremely difficult for an enemy warship to target the brain of the operation and instead enabled the crew to endure a withering barrage of enemy fire before becoming ineffective or unable to influence a particular battle. With most of their systems automated, the ship's exterior required very little manning and could thus operate effectively, despite taking massive damage to its hull, without influencing the life-sustaining systems that were secured behind hundreds of meters of armored plating.

While he performed most of his day to day work in his quarters, a room just off the bridge, Gemini remained in his command post when he had to command his fleet, track a battle, or send and receive updates both to their ministry of defense and from his subordinate commanders. Officers lined the walls and filled the center of the triangular room to monitor weather, space anomalies, defensive beacons, combat readiness, and logistical efforts. Gemini's chair was in the back of the triangle, faced a large viewing screen, and was elevated slightly, with thick armrests and computer systems on either side.

The screen itself was advanced enough to provide constant visual updates for everyone on the bridge by using a variety of smaller viewing screens imbedded in the larger one. Drone and scout cameras captured refugee efforts while up-to-date status bars showed him his crew strength, battle readiness, and a map displaying the location of the remainder of the Mateen fleets.

Castor, seated to his right, pressed a few buttons on his computer to bring up an image that displayed the Jarkian battleship and began to explain the situation. "We are starting to believe Casika's story a bit more," he began. "Brokk's ship seems to have originated from the Tassian system, specifically their home world."

Castor pressed a second button and the screen revealed a plotted map of the vessel's wormhole signature. "As you know, we have a few hours where the closing wormhole creates a warped version of space. This display you see now is the trail of warped space where the ship traveled from to arrive at its destination." Gemini nodded and Castor continued, "We also have data that was retrieved from one of our beacons indicating two massive explosions in the subspace surrounding Rodam immediately before Casika's vessel exited the wormhole and crashed. This indicates that they were fired upon but certainly isn't as concrete as our previous assumptions. It's possible that there were simply engine malfunctions that caused the explosions. We're leaning toward torpedoes though, based on the splatter in the subspace." Castor switched the screen again to zoom in around a portion of space above Rodam that provided the reason for their analysis. Like a silk web wet and visible from dew in the early morning, the fabric of subspace was disturbed and contorted. "This type of splatter is consistent with short range torpedoes—"

"But it doesn't explain Brokk's legitimacy to do so," Gemini cut in. "If indeed he was tracking a fugitive vessel seeking to make it back to its home planet first, it would be reasonable for him to originate from there and then chase them further once they refused to be boarded."

"True, but there's more," retorted Castor. "As with our ability to track this battleship's origin, when all wormholes are created, a massive amount of negative energy is formed around the space and lasts residually for quite some time. Well, we've detected hundreds of isolated spots of negative energy deposits around Tassi." He paused. "I mean literally hundreds of them."

"So what does that mean?" asked Gemini, realizing the probable answer as soon as he asked it.

"Artillery," Castor answered. "It looks like there has been an interstellar artillery barrage going on for at least fifteen hours."

"Fifteen hours?" asked a shocked Gemini, then followed up with a flurry of other questions. "Did anyone alert us while I was on Rodam? Why hasn't the Galactic Council notified us? How on earth could the Jarks be responsible for waging a war without us knowing?"

Castor shrugged and gave him a sheepish smile. "This is just our analysis. It may turn out to have flaws—"

"No." Gemini said, interrupting him again. "Don't sell our crew short. Alert the fleet and bring up three destroyers to support our discussions. Keep them behind the moon, hidden by its magnetic field," he said to Castor. "I'm going to talk to Casika."

Gemini flew out of his seat and through the door of the bridge. While he could have taken a magnetized horizontal lift system to shuttle himself to the medical bay, but Gemini preferred to stretch out his legs from the morning's hike. He could already feel them tightening, and it would give him more time to think.

***

Gemini found Casika resting in one of the recovery rooms. Her wounds had been treated and were already halfway healed, while the larger cuts were covered in white bandages. She had been given a white robe and was wearing a monitor attached to her finger. A screen displayed her vitals, and when Gemini entered the room, her heart rate spiked on the screen as she sat up.

"I don't look that intimidating, do I?" Gemini joked, offering her a smile from behind his stony face.

Casika smiled and looked a bit embarrassed. "You've been very kind to me," she responded. "I feel almost a hundred percent better. And look," she said with a smile, gesturing down at her arm. "It's not broken!"

"That's fantastic," Gemini said warmly as he sat down in a chair adjacent to her bed. "You owe our Creator your deepest thanks; His preservation of you was a miracle."

Her long white hair rested gently on the pillow, and she returned her gaze to the ceiling. Seeing her youth and vigor, Gemini couldn't keep from being intrigued by her and had to force himself to continue his barrage of questions from earlier rather than engage in small talk. "I need you to explain in detail what happened on the planet before you fled."

Casika fixed her eyes on the ceiling and fiddled her thumbs together. "There were explosions, giant explosions from the center of the city. Bombs fell from the sky and were hitting everywhere. I was running for the airfield, trying to escape, and I remember looking up and seeing this streak of white, almost like a sky taxi pushing through clouds. It's so strange, but I remember it so clearly, this white streak against our blue sky. It fell, and as I was running I was thinking, *This is going to hit me.* But I couldn't change directions. I had to keep running. The next thing I remember, I was on the transport ship. Someone must have pulled me aboard."

"What happened next?"

"We were crammed so tight and everything happened so fast, it's hard to say. But the ship was banking and rolling. This man standing above me kept falling into me and leaning against my arm. I wanted to speak to him, but it was too loud. I couldn't hear much. I thought I heard cannon fire outside, but the engines were too loud. Then, right as we made the jump into the wormhole, a massive explosion twisted us." She paused and her eyes went down to watch her hands as she played with her fingers. Gemini could see tears form, but she fought them back and looked back up at him. "That's really all I remember before the crash."

"What did you do before the attack?" Gemini asked.

"I was a vagrant…sometimes waited tables. It was a holiday." A hint of a smile molded her expression as she remembered back to her drink. "I stole some guys drink off the beach. Broke it on my leg during the attack. I was so mad that the guy had more than I did. It's silly to be so mad over something so simple. But I was. I guess he probably dead now." She fell silent as tears formed again in her eyes, but this time she couldn't fight them back and instead she allowed them to fall to her cheeks.

Gemini stood to leave, but Casika stopped him by grabbing his huge hand in protest. "Thank you for saving me," she said. "I thought I was doomed."

He smiled to her. "Get some rest." He said as he exited the room and hurried back toward the bridge.

CHAPTER EIGHT

Despite initial problems with the blockade, Brokk was pleased to learn that the remainder of the invasion was going extremely well. Lago's battle group had achieved air superiority in relatively short fashion on Tassi and was able to maneuver his destroyers to initiate a blockade of Tassi's second inhabited planet, Krellen. With air superiority achieved, all three transport vessels had deployed millions of soldiers across the Tassian home world and were in the initial stage of rounding up remaining ground defenses and establishing order.

Despite small skirmishes, Brokk was even more pleased to learn that the invasion force was meeting little resistance. Out-matched, out-trained, and out-gunned, the Tassian defense force was surrendering in droves and negotiations were already underway for a ceasefire. In a mere twenty-four hours, the Jarks had managed to decimate the space fleet of the Tassian Empire, inflict massive causalities on the Tassian defense force, and would soon accept an unconditional surrender. Brokk would be praised as a war hero by his government and surely promoted to the rank of Senior Admiral for his actions. Ruling as Chancellor was well within his grasp.

The only barrier to Brokk's plan now existed in the form of a crashed transport vessel on a Mateen moon. If no one survived, it would be as simple as thanking the Mateens for their time and leaving their solar system. If, however, there were survivors, Brokk would have to convince the commander that these were criminals, and regardless of the story he was being told, there could be no compromise without a complete surrender of those criminals. This was the only way Brokk could ensure the Galactic Order remained uninvolved until he was ready to address them as the newly crowned Chancellor of the Tassian system.

As Brokk gamed the discussion in his head, he was interrupted by his pilot Terre in an incoming transmission. Looking up from his chair, he raised a finger to signal answering the call. Suddenly, the hideous image of a stony-skinned Mateen commander appeared on the screen. They were uglier than Brokk had imagined, and disdain for the species flooded his thoughts.

"Good morning!" Brokk answered cheerfully, composing himself from his initial shock. "I am Fleet Commander Brokk, Commander of the 9th Jarkian Space Fleet. I'm grateful you were able to engage with me on such short notice. I'm certain you've noticed a small vessel crashed onto your moon half a day ago. We've been pursuing it. There are fugitives aboard, and I'd like to recover the vessel."

He paused as he waited for his transmission to be fully translated into the ear of the Mateen. At last, a smile appeared on the stony man's face, and he returned his own greeting. "Good morning to you as well, Commander Brokk. I'm Gemini. We've already recovered the bodies from the crash site and the ship itself. They looked like civilians, and my men didn't discover any contraband. For what reasons were you pursuing them?"

Despite the commander's response that indicated the Mateens were not going to allow a search, Brokk drove forward. "These Tassians are wanted by my government for a terrorist plot against our people. We have been chasing them since they were on our home world. Upon traveling to Tassi, we tried to apprehend them, but when they tried to escape their own planet upon learning of us, we intercepted their vessel using force in accordance with intergalactic law. I mean you no inconvenience, Commander. We'll be happy to help your team with recovery efforts so we can take control of their vessel and exploit it for additional intelligence about their terrorist activities." Brokk feigned a smile but dropped it flat after only a few seconds. He hated politics; hated the Mateens even more.

"Our research, Commander Brokk, indicates that you've merely been pursuing them from the Tassian home world and not from Jark, at least within the last few hours of this chase. Out of curiosity, what plot did you uncover, and just how dangerous could the women and children on board have been?"

Brokk fumed in the midst of this disrespectful Mateen commander. Everyone wrote off the Jarks as an isolated and inconsequential race in the Galactic Order, and the Mateens were no different. Surely this Mateen Commander saw his own hypocrisy. He would never have questioned the motives of another race. It was only the Jarks who were guilty until proven innocent. Among other things, conquering the Tassian home world would give the Jarks the respect they deserved and launch them onto the galactic scene, where they could begin dictating future events. "All Tassians are wanted by the Jark government," Brokk responded resentfully. "A failure to comply with our search and recovery of the vessel will be viewed as a hostile act against our people."

Gemini smiled widely angering Brokk even more. *Insolent Mateen.* "You would view us as committing a hostile act for simply maintaining our sovereign borders and questioning your purpose within our sovereign system?"

"We would view you as taking sides with a dangerous and insulting enemy to the Jark home world!" Brokk snarled, finally losing his temper.

"I'll comply on three conditions, Commander Brokk," Gemini said as he rose from his chair. "Explain to me and the Galactic Council why you are shelling the Tassian home world without a formal declaration of war or any provocation on behalf of the Tassian people, explain why you didn't approach the counselor for approval prior to war, and explain just how long you plan to occupy their land. Then, I will let you search in accordance with intergalactic law, assuming the Galactic Council agrees with your right to search our moon."

Brokk remained seated while he considered his response. Neither calm discussion nor threatening was going anywhere, and the commander's last statement indicated that the Mateens had already learned about the invasion. Someone must have survived the crash from the vessel below.

"Do you see my golden skin, Gemini?" Brokk asked at last, standing and rolling up his sleeve to expose his forearm while walking towards the display screen. "There was certainly provocation on the behalf of all Tassians, and my skin proves I am a descendant of the rightful heir to the planet. Any Tassian left alive is an offense to my people, and you risk putting yours directly into the center of our wrath." Brokk rolled his sleeve down and settled back into his chair. "I'll give you one galactic day to consider handing over the survivors for imprisonment. If you refuse, you will be viewed as an enemy of our people."

"I don't need a day," Gemini retorted. "The survivor of your mad campaign has been granted permanent refuge with my people. Under the strongest possible terms I urge you to end your assault on Tassi and return to Jark. The lives of millions of Tassians will be on your head if you misstep, and the Galactic Council will be getting a full report."

Brokk shut the screen off and ordered his crew to jump them back to Tassi. He suspected that Gemini knew the Galactic Council would take weeks to deliberate on any action against the Jarks, but it was insulting enough to threaten him with the act, let alone attempt to lecture him on the morality of warfare.

Regardless, Brokk knew he would need to accelerate his plans to isolate the Tassians and demand their surrender. Only with their surrender would he be able to stave off an attempt at pushing the Jarks back to their home world—and Brokk would never go back. They were too close to victory.

Fuming, he called Lago using the PTS. *I need you to develop plans to defeat a counterattack. I'll put Commander Hess in charge of the ground invasion.* And with those words sent through the brain link, he also sent the fury of emotions that gave Lago enough background in mere seconds.

***

Gemini didn't need to communicate to anyone. Like a cloud of witnesses, the entire planet had tuned into his conversation with the Jarkian Fleet Commander and rallied behind him in support. They weren't physically behind him of course, but even in the void of space, the presence of trillions of Mateens could be felt passionately reaching out and reassuring their military leader. He found comfort in their support, but their reassurance of his judgements left a heavy burden on the commander to make the right decisions for the people he swore to protect. Gemini knew he would have to be very careful while toeing the line between strength and diplomacy to ensure he wasn't the one who took the wrong step.

After some reflection, Gemini decided that it was time to visit Casika again. He didn't know enough about the feud between the Jarks and the Tassians and found himself wondering what he may have just stumbled into. Brokk's claims to the Tassian throne were worrisome, and determining if this was an isolated invasion with legitimacy was his top priority.

While the Mateens were overly empathetic, they were also

isolationists. In order to determine their involvement, the entire race would have to understand the situation that the Tassians faced. If Gemini's investigation did find that the Tassians were innocent in the clutches of a megalomaniac, chances were good the Mateens would intervene, if not for their own selfish reasons. If, however, the Tassians had participated in an exchange of punches before this event, then there was good chance that the Mateens would remain neutral. They had no interest in the affairs of other races that did not personally affect their own well-being. Gemini sighed as he considered the Mateen doctrines of containment, realizing that they were never black and white.

Don't worry, Castor said through the cloud of bystanders. *We got you.*

***

Gemini arrived to find Casika moving about the medical bay, speaking with his staff. Her recovery was quick, which he attributed to her youth, and she looked to be comfortable in her new environment. As he approached, he could tell that she had asked his medical officer to explain the different systems they used to diagnose patients wounded from a battle.

Typically, Gemini always enjoyed hearing his officers boast about their systems. Sadly, his needs today were infinitely more urgent. Gemini cleared his throat and stepped into the conversation. "Sorry Tor," he said to his chief of Medical Operations, "I'm going to have to talk to her privately for a few minutes." Tor smiled and took a step back to cheerfully oblige his commander the opportunity.

"Would you join me in my quarters, Casika?" he asked, placing a hand on her back and extending the other toward the passageway door that led toward the bridge and his private office and quarters. She nodded, and Gemini led her out of the medical bay and down the ship's white-walled corridors, decorated with photos of the oceans, forests, and cliffs of the Mateen home world.

"So you're in charge of this whole ship?" Casika asked, acting impressed as they walked down the brightly lit steel-floored passageway.

"I am," he responded with a chuckle. "Are you impressed?"

"I am," she replied, mimicking him. "You have a remarkable medical bay." She paused, but Gemini could tell that she wasn't done speaking. "I just can't imagine what would have happened to me if I hadn't been found by you, if I hadn't been treated on this ship. I'm extremely grateful to you for my life."

Gemini smiled. "Life is extremely important to us," he explained. "When one of our brothers is injured, we all feel it. And I don't mean in the theoretical sense. We are deeply affected by the pain and anguish of a comrade and experience each death with the one who is dying. This way," he said, leading her down another corridor. "We have put a lot of resources into ensuring we maximize life's chances whenever possible."

Casika seemed shocked. "How do you...feel it?"

"We're telepaths," he said, suddenly realizing that she must not have known initially. "All of us are continually connected."

Casika took a moment to process what he had just told her and then frowned. "All the time? Like, even when you want privacy?"

"It's not quite like that," he chuckled. "I can choose to prevent people from experiencing my feelings or reading my thoughts. My mind is still my own, but we generally like to remain open to one another. Telepathy is a sense that is just as important as sight or touch, and it forms inseparable bonds within our race."

"It must be hard, then, to lose someone," she said. Her golden eyes dimmed a bit, and Gemini suspected she was remembering holding the dying woman's hand on the ship. "I couldn't imagine feeling their anguish as they died," she finally said. "And the fear..." she added.

Gemini entered his office first and pulled out a chair for his guest. "Sometimes it's nice for us to be there to take away their fear," he responded, moving to the opposite side of his desk. As a fleet commander, he was expected to be able to provide a lavish meeting room for any guests he might be required to entertain. His office offered a small part of that for smaller, more private visits and was complete with a beautiful deep orange-and-red hand-carved desk from a Llexya tree native to his home planet.

Taking her seat, Casika's smaller frame looked preposterous as it sunk into the chair built for the much larger Mateen race. As Gemini sat down opposite from her, he peered over his desk to check if her feet even touched the floor. She noticed, and a surprised giggle came out of her mouth as she pulled her legs up and crossed them underneath her body. Casika's vibrant golden eyes contrasted sharply with the shockingly white hair that draped itself over her shoulders. The radiant sparkle on her skin gave the appearance of glitter sprinkled from the heavens above.

Whenever Gemini met a new race in the galaxy, he always found himself shocked at how eerily similar they all were. Other than skin color, skin texture, and body size, which were largely a result of atmospheric and environmental conditions, the known sentient life forms throughout the galaxy remained virtually the same. This incredible similarity led many philosophers to claim one Supreme Being as responsible for all of creation. Others seemed to believe that evolution had simply resulted in the optimal form of life across many planets in many environments at the same time. They posit that because all known life is made up of essentially the same building blocks, there should be no surprise that it followed similar evolutionary paths.

Still, Gemini had to side with the creator theory and considered himself a deep and genuine believer in a creator God. The similarities between the races and the immense quantity of information stored within their genetic code were overwhelming evidence in his opinion. As before, he found himself stunned at those same similarities in the solitary Tassian survivor sitting in front of him.

Gemini opened a black-handled drawer from his extravagant desk and removed a small orb. The circular object was dark silver with evenly spaced indents all around it. He gently squeezed it and then opened his palm, releasing the ball to hover over the right side of the desk. Soon, it hummed and produced a holographic white screen in front of them both.

"Are you familiar with this?" Gemini asked.

Casika, looking shocked, shook her head no.

He laughed. "Well, you have nothing to worry about. This is a device that will help record our conversation for official record. As you tell your side of the story, it will reproduce the facts against the information we have in our database to present a comprehensive picture of the history surrounding the invasion of your home world and of our meeting each other.

"We Mateens are visual and corporate learners. The orb will essentially turn your version of history into a digestible movie and help us to educate our race. The aspects you don't know or don't say will be populated with the orb's best guess. Events will be chronologically organized using our analysis of your ship's journey, and a comprehensive picture will be formed for us all."

Gemini paused to look at the door and then returned his eyes to Casika. "Your testimony could be the difference in our decision on whether or not to intervene, Casika, and I should also warn you—it could be the difference in you saving your home world or being placed on trial for treason if we commit our forces based on intentional falsehoods. This isn't to be taken lightly and we are very good at detecting lies."

Casika's face fell flat as Gemini allowed his disclaimer to soak in. While Gemini would rather not have to provide such a disclaimer, the Mateen lawyers demanded that the interviewee be aware of what was at stake. Whenever he performed one of these interviews, Gemini always hoped that he had established a relationship beforehand that would allow a person to speak openly, despite the consequences for lying. "Shall we begin?" he said at last with a smile.

CHAPTER NINE

The jump back to Tassi took approximately six minutes. In that time, Brokk's ship skipped over thousands of stars as they folded space from one point to the next. Brokk was one of the few captains in the Jarkian fleet who enjoyed watching the process on his monitor on the deck of the ship. The screen captured the stars as ghastly apparitions glowing in the darkness; as soon as someone saw and tried to focus on a point of light, the star stretched and faded out of view and was replaced with thousands more. At other times, the cameras captured the blackest parts of space that anyone had ever seen and sent shudders down the commander's neck when he realized a good mechanic was the only thing keeping him and his entire crew from becoming entirely consumed from that very emptiness that they tried to hop over.

Following his interaction with the Mateen fleet commander, Brokk decided his force needed to deploy sensor and counter beacons further from the Tassian system to expand their defensive perimeter. While the sensors simply identified and relayed information about oncoming vessels, they worked in concert with counter beacons. These counter beacons disrupted the energy that existed in the subspace in a way that defeated a ship's ability to conduct wormhole travel. Essentially, they dissipated the exotic energy that was formed during travel and ensured that if a Mateen fleet did arrive, it would have to cross the solar system conventionally rather than jumping past the Jarkian defenses as the Jarks had done previously to the Tassians. The technology was a trade-off. For Tassi to employ the beacons meant that they would have to forfeit the profits that they gained from easy tourism. Conversely, however, their greed had left them entirely open to a surprise attack. Brokk wouldn't make that same mistake.

After inspecting his new defensive layers, Brokk took a shuttle to join Lago on the planet's surface. The descent through the atmosphere of the Tassian home world was stunning. Brokk had never seen such beauty, especially when compared to Jark, the planet his people were forced to inhabit as a result of Tassian injustice.

Instead of fiery red skies, the atmosphere was a rich blue dashed with fluffy white clouds. Green trees and foliage covered the ground, while green pastures stretched far beyond the city limits. Oceans sparkled and reflected the pure white light that beamed down from the two suns that encircled the planet.

As he neared the megacity that enveloped nearly all of Tassi, Brokk could see smoke rising into the sky from simmering hulks of destroyed Tassian military vehicles and anti-aircraft weapons; once inside the city limits, however, his forces had managed to harm little infrastructure, and what appeared to have been previously burning had been long extinguished.

The shuttle landed on a small pad atop a Tassian government building. The building was a crystal glass masterpiece that shot nearly forty stories into the sky. From the shuttle pad, Brokk was able to look directly down through the glass and into the magnificent structure below. Light from the suns penetrated the clear crystal walls on each side, illuminating the office space, while the crystals themselves separated and magnified the full spectrum of color, enabling those colors to dance back and forth in brilliant reds, blues, yellows, and greens. More impressive than that was the fact that Brokk could actually stare straight down the forty stories directly into a pool of clear water below.

Lago appeared at a covered entryway on the corner of the roof and called out to greet the commander. "What do you think of your new office space, Commander Brokk?" he shouted, smiling.

Brokk turned and strolled toward him, his entourage of guards in tow. "It's fit for a king," he called back warmly. Meeting halfway, the two turned toward the sea and gazed across the horizon. One sun slowly sunk to the west, shooting rays across a glistening ocean, as the second hovered above them as if it were high noon. "So this will be our view every morning?" he asked.

"Every morning, evening, and midday," Lago responded. "I don't think the view will ever change." Lago shifted and used his arms to support his heavy torso against the crystal rooftop. Despite the gravity being much weaker on Tassi as it was on Jark, Lago's habits would likely never leave him. Squinting a bit, he looked up to his commander and remarked, "The white sun really causes you to shimmer, Brokk."

Brokk looked down at his golden arms and held them out to his front. They were much lighter than they had been on Jark, and they even sparkled a bit as he moved them back and forth in the sunlight. Brokk smiled. He finally began to look like the royalty he deserved to be. "This used to be the kings' palace, no?" he asked Lago, still fixated on his own complexion.

Lago nodded. "Dating all the way back to King Autarieus, but let's ask our prisoners for the detailed history. I think you will be interested in speaking to Chancellor Ebb yourself."

Brokk's heart fluttered when he heard those words. "You've already captured Chancellor Ebb?" he said, astonished. Not in his wildest dreams did Brokk imagine they would have so quickly captured the leader of the Tassian government.

"He refused to go into hiding," Lago responded with a shrug. "When our soldiers arrived outside of the building, the chancellor and a group of delegates walked outside with their hands up, demanding to speak to the leader of the invasion. Following his surrender, the commander of the Tassian forces simply fled from the city, withdrawing his forces to the outskirts. I'm certain that he'll accept our terms for surrender, but with so few fighters and even fewer vehicles, they are nothing to worry about."

Lago led Brokk down the crystal stairs of the government building and into Chancellor Ebb's office. Light beamed brilliantly through the walls and danced in a full spectrum of color as the crystal filtered the rays and magnified them inside the building. Seated in a crystal chair behind a light silver desk and under the guard of Jarkian soldiers was Ebb, the soon-to-be-ousted ruler of Tassi. As Brokk entered, Ebb rose to his feet, not to give honor, but to impose his authority. He was a tall, skinny man who wore a scowl on his face. Like Brokk's, his skin also glistened in the sun's light and emanated a soft, golden glow. Brokk suspected he had royal roots but didn't let that deter his own legitimacy from the seat that Ebb currently occupied.

"What is the meaning of this invasion?" Ebb thundered. The guards in the room stepped toward him, but Brokk shut them down with the wave of his hand. Instead of lashing out against the pale-skinned leader, Brokk moved to one of two chairs opposite the chancellor's desk and sat down, gesturing with an open palm for Ebb to do the same.

Ebb refused. "How dare you attack our sovereign planet on the celebration of a holy day!" he bellowed. "Do you have any idea what the Galactic Council will do to you and your people when they find out about this? None of this will fly. None of it!"

Brokk remained seated for a little longer, taking time to examine his foe. He couldn't read minds, but he could sense courage and fear. Ebb had a little of both, but it was his fear that interested Brokk. The ease at which Brokk managed to sweep across the Tassian defenses and capture the chancellor previously caused him to worry that they had fallen into a trap. The stench of fear, however, helped to reassure Brokk that the Tassians had no such trap planned because if there was one, Brokk would have sensed a smugness about the chancellor. There was none.

"I know all about your holy day, Ebb." Brokk finally responded shortly. "You celebrate the day King Autarieus united the planet by exiling his family to Jark so that they might die for his own mistakes, do you not?"

"We celebrate the day that God, through a divine miracle, healed our planet, forgave our King, and united its people. Part of that healing was the banishment of the wicked half son, born out of adultery," Ebb retorted. "What interest do you have in our four thousand-year-old history anyway? Surely Jark hasn't decided to wage a fool's war over an exiled Tassian."

"Where is the king's line now?" Brokk asked through clenched teeth, promising himself not to lose his temper. "How did you get to become chancellor and skip past the holy line of King Autarieus? I can tell by your skin that you aren't full-blood royalty."

"That line disappeared hundreds of years ago," Ebb exclaimed. We elect our rulers democratically now—for the common good! What is the purpose of your invasion and why are you killing my people?"

"I demand unconditional surrender of your forces and a public statement yielding to Jarkian rule over your planet. I expect a peaceful transition and a systematic disarming of your military. Your people will be allowed to live on this planet under the condition that they swear allegiance to the Jarkian Empire, and you will personally be allowed to continue to exist if you swear allegiance to me, your new chancellor." Brokk paused to take a breath. "Those are my terms."

"They will never accept them!" Ebb shouted. "Our government is owned by the people! You are mad. The Galactic Council will never accept them! You'll only bring sorrow and embarrassment to your home world. I implore you to end your mad campaign!"

Brokk stretched his open palm out to his side and Lago placed a rolled-up charter into it. Standing, Brokk thrust the document at Chancellor Ebb. "I am a direct descendant of King Autarieus, banished to the Jark home world for something my ancestors had no decision in. If any laws were broken, they were broken by the king himself. I have returned to claim Tassi as the rightful heir to the king's throne, to clear my ancestral line and our good name, and to ensure that my ancestors are remembered as persecuted and not despised as heathens.

"The Galactic Council will side with my claim and will have your illegitimate shadow government executed for unlawfully seizing the throne. You have twenty-four hours to sign that document, or I'll have you sign it in your own blood." Brokk motioned his guards to come forward and take a hold of Ebb. "Throw him into jail with the rest of the government officials you have rounded up. After twelve hours, we'll begin executing an official every hour until he signs my charter." Brokk looked back to Ebb as he was being led out of the room. "The lives of your people are in your hands."

CHAPTER TEN

"Then dig them faster," Remmel bellowed at his officers from inside the hastily prepared operations center. Looking around the table, he saw fresh faces that had never tasted victory or defeat, ones that had never even experienced the brutality of a land battle. Remmel was an old soldier. He had been around long enough to have participated in what scholars called *the last land war*, and he had seen the sheer brutality of it. While massive space fleets and their commanders got the glory from society for acting as deterrents to end all wars, Remmel had continued to prepare his dwindling group of ground pounders for the fierceness of war and the gruesomeness of the acts they would commit against other living creatures.

For his part, Remmel was commended and promoted to the rank of senior ground commander. Now, however, looking across his assembled officers as they crouched in a dark green tent on the edge of the city, he found himself doubting their training, and ultimately, their resolve. Remmel stood and dismissed his men. They had his orders. Dig in, camouflage the remaining anti-aircraft weapons and armored vehicles, and prepare for a counterattack. All departed but one: his son. In the presence of his only son, Remmel let his guard down and eventually began to weep. The two stood in silence, listening to the hammering of pickaxes and the slicing of shovels.

"I can only do what the last war and my studying have taught me," the old commander eventually said through broken and shaky words. "I fear we've already failed you."

"Nobody doubts your leadership, Dad," the man responded, moving in front of him. For too long, Remmel viewed Cale as just a boy, his son, but still just a boy. Now, in the darkness of the tent and from the dirtiness of his uniform, he realized that Cale was a man— and not just a man, but a commander with his own troop.

"If we fight, if we have to take back the city, I will need you to convince the men to give everything. To give it their all so that future generations can benefit." Remmel insisted, not sure if the training had hardened his unit for this one ultimate ending.

"They'll fight." Cale responded.

"Your generation has never seen war! You haven't seen how terrible it will be." He paused and shifted his weight uncomfortably, guilty that he couldn't keep his emotions under control. Remmel took his eyes off of his son and gazed to the draping cloth roof that they shamefully called their command center. "I still wake up, you know. Sometimes I think I'm still on that river; that beautiful river with the white and pink pebbles. But I realize there's a rifle in my hand, and suddenly, someone else is there too…" Remmel trailed off and looked up at Cale to see if he was still following him. Cale was. "I always kill him," he finished, knowing Cale understood.

"They'll fight, Dad," Cale said again. "We haven't seen the horrors, you're right, but we love this city, this planet. We'll all fight to the death." He paused as if choosing his next words carefully. "You need to rest," he finally said, turning to leave.

Cale walked out of the tent, leaving Remmel alone to consider this final great battle before him. Instead, he could think only of the past. He had fought for many things and all of them were things that he believed in, but never had he fought for the very survival of his people.

As Remmel himself stepped outside, a crisp breeze rushed through his wavy gray hair, and small drops of water fell from the sky, slowly at first, but gradually picking up speed. Because of the two suns, it didn't rain often on Tassi, but when it did, the skies dropped buckets. Remmel pulled his olive-green hood over his head and patrolled his lines. In spite of his son's advice, Remmel knew that rest wasn't what he needed. He needed a miracle, and while he waited, he would walk along his fighting positions instead.

The only places that the Tassians didn't expand their city were the low wetlands that took up about ten percent of the planet. These nasty areas were filled with insects and amphibians of all sizes, as well as larger predatory animals that lived on the outskirts of the city while feeding off the trash and occasionally hunting in the marsh for prey. Remmel had calculated that he could feed his army for a few months by simply scavenging for food, but if there was no quick resolution to this invasion, he feared surrender would be their only option. There was another reason, however, that Remmel had chosen this place. The wetlands were the sewage grounds for the entire planet. This would be the last place the enemy would search for him, and thus, it was the best place he could think of to hide an army.

Everywhere he walked, men cleared the ground of brush, dug trenches, and built barricades. Thorny briars speckled the landscape, and many of the soldiers worked hard to pull them up and line the trenches with their nasty two inch spikes. Ahead of the trench, soldiers strung laser wire and placed mines. Within just a few hours, the pristine world that had come together to celebrate the uniting of their planet became a battle zone; the plants, Remmel presumed, would thrive from the nutrients in his soldiers' bones.

As rain fell, the ground refused to swallow any more. Puddles formed and the boots of thousands of soldiers turned their camp from grass to mud. Trenches filled with water, but Remmel's men ignored it and continued to dig. This was the last defense of Tassi, and along with forty thousand men, this was where Remmel planned to meet his enemy.

CHAPTER ELEVEN

"You'll have to start over, Casika. None of us will understand this." Gemini was getting agitated and shifted his large body in his brown-backed leather chair. None of her claims made any sense. The Mateens of all people understood the intensity of a corporate memory, but to claim that this feud between Brokk and Tassi went back thousands of years sounded absurd. It didn't just sound absurd. To Gemini, it was absurd.

Casika, too, appeared agitated and uncomfortable, but Gemini didn't suspect that she was outright lying. This was the trouble with history—it was always taught by someone with a subjective perspective. The orb was developed to help with objectivity and memory. It had the ability to incorporate feelings and emotions into the history that those emotions so richly experienced. The orb made history living, but while it was meant to capture history as it was occurring, it too had trouble applying logic to stories not told from an objective perspective; stories that sounded more like folklore and fairy tales.

Gemini swirled to one side in his chair and stood up. Casika, whose eyes were half glazed over from exhaustion, startled from the sudden motion. "Where are you going?" she demanded, hope fading from her face as she surmised that his standing up meant that the session was over.

"I think we've done enough for one day," he replied as he strode toward the door and motioned with his hand for it to open. "You're exhausted from the crash, I'm exhausted from my trip, and I still have to review what you've already told me."

"We can't stop now!" she implored. "You have to believe me. You have to believe us! This was unprovoked. He's bitter and jealous. You saw it yourself with his golden skin. We all learn about it in school. All of us do. But nobody thought…nobody thought they would actually attack us. Nobody." She had worked herself up out of her chair and had come to within a few feet of the gray-skinned fleet commander. "My people are dying. They are dying trying to defend our peaceful planet. We've done nothing, we've done nothing!"

Gemini stopped her by putting his heavy hand on her shoulder. His crimson eyes flared as he debated his response. It was rare that anyone ever disputed him on anything. *How could she not see his compassion toward her? How could she attack him as the bad guy?*

The collective mind always understood his motives, and if they didn't, all he had to do was open them up to a glimpse of his perspective and the discussion would end. It always ended. This irrational Tassian surely understood his predicament. *Could she honestly expect him to wage war with the Jarks without understanding the situation? Could she really expect him to launch a full-scale counterattack after a little girl's history lesson and a megalomaniac's skin color?*

He suspected not, and yet she pressed him. "Casika," he responded calmly, "I cannot send my men to die without ensuring that this is a moral endeavor. We must understand the situation. I have contacted the Galactic Council and have dispatched my own scouts to your home world. If the war is not being conducted in accordance with galactic law, the Council will intervene, but you must allow us to deliberate and to exhaust diplomacy."

She brushed his hand from her shoulder and walked out of the door and into the arms of her escorts who had been waiting to take her to her room. "While you deliberate, my people die," she said coldly, refusing to look into his eyes.

Gemini stood for a moment longer, collecting his thoughts. Suddenly, he became aware of the orb humming quietly behind him. It had captured the whole exchange, measured her heart rate, and analyzed her pupils and body language, and would order it all in a way that made sense to his people. He would rewatch all that the orb had captured several times tonight as he organized the events in his own mind before presenting it to the council. *The outcast half-breed son of an ancient king…would he truly go to war over such distant history? What claim could he honestly have for the throne?* And suddenly, the most important question of all came into Gemini's mind: *What would he do to the people he believed had betrayed him if all of this was true?*

"We've reached the Tassian system," Castor said from behind, interrupting Gemini's train of thought. Gemini turned to see him but didn't answer. "Has she given you what you needed?" Castor asked, trying to get him to acknowledge his presence.

"Have you deployed our scouts?" Gemini finally responded, changing the subject so overtly that he caught Castor momentarily off guard.

"Yes, but our sensors are ineffective. They are using blocking beacons to keep us from finding out what is happening on the planet's surface."

"And the scouts?" Gemini asked again.

"They're through the initial sensors, but it will take a while. They have to be very deliberate about where they can go to avoid detection. We can't communicate with them beyond the beacons, so they'll have to return to us before we learn anything." Castor's expression suggested that he hoped the last part was all right. Commanders never liked it when they couldn't communicate with an element on the battlefield, but the desire for information was infinitely greater than any associated risks.

Finally, Gemini smiled to relieve his old friend. He himself had started as a scout and envied the squad commander in charge. His task had been simple and very little rode on his ultimate success.

There were only seven rules to being a scout, and Gemini slowly recited them in his head. *Gain and maintain contact with the enemy, always orient on the recon objective, never leave reconnaissance in reserve, retain freedom of maneuver, develop the situation rapidly…*Gemini stopped, realizing Castor was staring at him again, waiting for a response. Embarrassed, he was relieved that he had kept these last thoughts private, as subordinates dared not enter the mind of a commander without being invited in.

Since Casika had boarded the ship, Gemini found himself in several places at once, unable to fully focus on the present and constantly reaching back into the past. Her youth mesmerized him and the prospect of war thrilled him. He would never admit it to the Mateen collective, but he fancied himself built for war, and this high-stakes game of chess made him feel just as youthful and alive as the Tassian survivor he had rescued a few orbits earlier.

"Make sure no one goes to the planet's surface," he finally responded. "I want information on the Jarkian fleet, their approximate ground force strength in the city, and a detailed analysis from our staff that composes their strengths and weaknesses as opposed to our own. Lastly, figure out if there are any reserve or rebel forces remaining on the planet. Our ability to gather information and continue to gain an understanding of the situation before taking action is paramount." Gemini put his hand on Castor's shoulder to reassure him. "This is what we live for, is it not, Castor?"

His executive officer nodded and smiled. Castor's gray skin formed black wrinkles on his cheeks as his parting lips revealed pure white teeth behind his stony complexion. Castor turned to walk out and then stopped. "Oh, I almost forgot. You have a message from some senator on the Council of Cultural Affairs for the Galaxy. I can't remember his home world, but I thought it was odd that it wouldn't be a member of the Security Council, don't you?"

Gemini scrunched his face in part disbelief and part curiosity. "I guess we'll find out," he said, returning to his desk to check the message. Galactic politics never made much sense to Gemini, but then again, they didn't make much sense to his entire race. The Mateens were as much an isolationist empire as any in the galaxy. Politics, trade, and expansionism were of far less interest to his people than were isolationism and planetary defense. The Mateens would rather miss out on the experience of a thousand different cultures than to let down their guard and watch their home world burn. Contentment with what he already had, he believed, was the true answer to peace.

Objectively speaking, the Tassian desire for openness and tourism had led to their downfall, and this mistake gave Gemini the perfect reason to remain resolute in this isolationist endeavor. Why would they ever desire to make friends or enemies of another race? No, neutrality had worked for a long time, and Gemini hoped that it would continue to do so. Still, a peaceful existence sometimes meant exterminating the wasps that built nests in your backyard, and as far as neighbors were concerned, the Tassians were the nearest ones.

***

Two large, gray-faced Mateens led Casika down a narrow corridor of the ship and into her new sleeping quarters. From what she could tell, the ship was mostly rectangular. It had two main corridors that ran the length of the ship and multiple sub-corridors that joined the main ones to a multitude of offices, facilities, and sleeping quarters. The ship itself was well lit and its interior was colored in light tans, whites, and browns. She could easily allow herself to believe that she was walking through a hotel lobby rather than a spaceship, but every fifty feet or so a massive window would appear, ripping her from the belief that she might be on Tassi, forcing her to instead come to grips with the fact that she was in the cold void of space that had become the final resting place for so many of her companions over the last day.

The three of them arrived at a door with a blue label on it. One of the men held his hand to the door, and it opened, revealing a large lobby that expanded at least three stories upward. There were a few people meandering around in the lobby, but it was generally quiet. "This is our guest hall," one of the escorts told her in a deep Mateen voice. "There is a restaurant on the main floor and an entertainment center here as well. On the upper level you will find the gym and living quarters. You are room 26B, meaning that you will go up these stairs," he said, pointing up a curved set of steps to her left, "and walk about halfway down the corridor. Please make yourself at home. If you need anything at all, simply find a Mateen in uniform and he will take care of you."

Casika tried to smile at the man as he left and, exhausted from her ordeal, looked around at her new residence. She even dared to call it *home* in her mind. *Home*, she thought again as she allowed herself to imagine that she could live comfortably and in peace here. Casika believed that she was near the back of the ship based on how they had walked here, but she truly had no idea. Two uniformed Mateen soldiers stood at the hall entryway she had just come through. Both were armed but appeared relaxed; one even chatted to a green-skinned female about the differences between fruits on various planets.

"Did you know a melon on Charlon can grow to the size of a car?" she asked him, touching his elbow as she smiled. He grinned, and Casika looked away to avoid the nausea that was growing inside of her. The green-skinned person, a Despone, was short and hairy and had thick legs and a torso to match. Despones were typically indentured servants on Tassi and she suspected elsewhere in the galaxy as well. Casika didn't know the Despone's back story, but she suspected that this woman was running from a similar life of servitude.

While the guards were Mateen, the guests in the lobby were from a variety of different places, all of them supposedly refugees seeking asylum on the Mateen home world. Some she recognized. A green-skinned male, presumably related to the female flirting with the guards, sat lazily on a chair, staring out of the window into the dark space beyond.

Beyond him, a red-haired three-foot-tall Pisky creature paced back and forth in one of the corners. Her people used to joke that the Piskies were the midgets of the galaxy, but in reality, Casika never met one whom she didn't like. She had served many of them back on Tassi and found them to be well-mannered and appreciative of her culture. Even now, as she stood awkwardly in the lobby, it was only the Pisky who didn't stare at her.

"Are any of these people dangerous?" she asked one of the guards at the door, offering a faint smile to cover her insecurities. The green-skinned woman sneered and walked away, making sure to show her utter distaste as she returned to her companion at the chair.

Casika's question, which the guard picked up on immediately, stemmed from a translucent-looking man in a chair near the center of the lobby. She could see the chair he rested on through his pale gray arms, and his face was nearly invisible, covered in a mask of his own dark brown hair. She had never seen anything like him before, and a shiver shot up her spine as she felt his eyes walk across her body.

"I wouldn't worry too much about them," he responded. "Most of these people have come to our solar system seeking asylum for one reason or another. We rarely turn anyone away, but it takes time to conduct a thorough investigation. While they wait, we keep them here. Besides, Mateen soldiers guard this portion of the ship all day and night. You have nothing to fear," he said reassuringly.

She thanked him but felt no more comfortable as she glanced past the man again. Instead of loitering, Casika hurried up the stairs toward her new quarters, maintaining a watchful eye around her as she did. The Pisky continued to pace until he was out of view, and she had to admit that he was kind of cute for being a full-grown, pink-skinned, and somewhat hairy creature.

Halfway down the hallway, Casika found her room. The door opened automatically as she approached, and it locked behind her after she entered. Somehow the computer system had known that it was her and not somebody who didn't belong, something they had surely preprogrammed while she had been in Gemini's office. Inside, the room was decorated beautifully, had ample floor space, a large bed, a wet bar stocked with glasses, and a reading area. Her bookshelves had already been loaded with the digital images of books and movies that, if she wanted to read or watch, she could simply drag a selection into her lap and it would materialize into usable content in an instant. In a corner near the window revealing the black abyss, a beautiful red-and-blue Mateen plant sat, emanating the warmth and life of a home world she had never visited but suddenly longed for. The plant's bright colors contrasted against the utter blackness of space and caused Casika to desperately wish the last twenty-four hours had been merely a nightmare.

If she couldn't wake up from the nightmare, she instead decided she would go to sleep. Grateful to lie down, Casika plopped her body flat on the bed and felt pain rush from the back of her head into her teeth. She still wasn't healed from the crash, but she was exhausted, and often that was the best form of anesthesia. Placing a hand on her head, she soon forgot all about her troubles and fell asleep.

CHAPTER TWELVE

Brokk groaned as he woke to the same simmering sunlight that tormented him in his new tower palace all night long. Even during the worst points of his previous battles, Brokk had always been able to find sleep when the time came to rest his head. Tassi, with its two stars and everlasting daylight, was the one exception. Overnight, Brokk mentally swore to hate this holy city and its inhabitants even more than he had the previous day.

As if reading his mind, Lago entered his room, and with a sly smile he asked "Why do we want this place again?" His face looked heavy and exhausted, as if he had even greater trouble sleeping than Brokk had. Even on that heavy face, however, Brokk's closest friend still had a way of cheering him up. The smirk showed a row of sharp, animalistic teeth that every pureblood Jark possessed, but it showed more than that. The smirk he wore demonstrated that there was little in the known universe that could keep Lago's pep and cheer from erupting up toward the surface.

Brokk greeted him with a warm smile, followed by a sigh of stale air from his lungs. Even though he never felt like he truly belonged on Jark, he found himself missing the hot sulfuric air and the dark red skies. Tassi was too bright, and instead of sulfur, all Brokk could smell was smog from the industrial city planet.

Turning from the window overlooking the ocean, he faced Lago. "It's been twelve hours. Has Ebb signed the ceasefire?"

"I'm afraid not," his dear friend responded. "Do you still want to move forward with the executions?"

"Absolutely," he answered resolutely. "This is the only way we can convince the Galactic Council to avoid an outright intervention. Bring two females from his cabinet to the roof along with Ebb and the charter. I'll execute them myself."

Lago exited his crystal room and descended the steps toward the makeshift prison. For a time, Brokk watched him through the walls, which were illuminated by the rays of the dual-helium suns that burned brightly above. After a while, Brokk shifted his gaze to the steps leading to the roof and decided to climb them. He wanted to pick a spot to throw the females from that made the greatest impact on the people watching below. Fear was Brokk's plan to quell any insurgency from forming in the midst of the governmental transition. It was a universal *law of the sword* that subjugated even the most unruly of people.

The law was simple: "I will keep killing you and your people until you submit to me. You will realize how helpless you are and, in utter desperation, will completely submit to my authority." Was it despotic? Yes. But Brokk didn't care. These people had betrayed his family millennia ago, and he was not going to show them mercy until they bowed to his reign.

From the roof, Brokk could see the streets of the entire capitol block of the city. To his east, patrols scanned houses for military deserters and weaponry. To his west, his soldiers were rounding up citizens to watch the transition of power unfold on his rooftop above. Behind him to the south, the gulf glistened as gentle waves danced back and forth against the beach. And most notably, to the north of his new palace, the sky was crowned with his very own battleship, taking watch over the entire planet and orchestrating his army's maneuvers.

Below the roof, as he again looked through the crystal floor, Brokk could see his guards escorting the party of three prisoners up the stairs. He moved to greet Ebb at the doorway. "Good morning, Ebb!" he bellowed. "How did you sleep last night?"

Ebb didn't respond. Instead, he kept his face down and his shoulders rolled forward in an attempt to comfort himself after a night of painful restraints attached to his hands and legs. Ebb didn't know it, but the nights would get worse if he didn't submit soon. Brokk allowed him to sleep only because he was being generous; the next step was a cell too narrow to sit and too cold to sleep.

Brokk squatted down and pushed his face close to Ebb's. "Did you sign the charter?" he snarled. Ebb didn't respond, and Brokk didn't expect him to. "Of course you didn't!" he shouted, stepping away from the chancellor and grabbing the prettier of the two Tassians by her long golden hair. The five-foot-tall female cabinet member let out a scream as he seized her. "And guess what, Ebb? It's been twelve hours!"

Brokk's large hand nearly engulfed the Tassian's head as he pulled her toward the edge of the roof. "What does she do for your government, Ebb?" he asked.

Finally, the chancellor lifted his eyes and spoke. "She is the secretary to our treasurer. She doesn't have anything to do with governance. She means nothing to you," he pleaded. His lips trembling and voice shook as he tried to find the words to turn Brokk's wrath. "What good does a charter do for you anyway, Brokk? You know the council will never accept it. They'll claim I was under duress!"

"So you'll sign it then?" Brokk retorted, bringing the now-crying Tassian close to the edge.

"It means nothing!" Ebb shouted back in desperation. "Please don't do this. Please don't. You can't come back from this!"

Brokk pushed her. He counted the number of seconds it took the girl to fall forty stories to the ground below. Finally, he heard a crunch and the crowd beneath him gasp and weep. "Bring me the next one," he ordered his guards, who now brought an older woman to his side. "How many people are going to die for a charter that means nothing to you, Ebb?" he questioned as he grabbed the arm of the next cabinet member. Tears streamed down her round face, but she didn't scream like the other victim, and barely a whimper exited her mouth. *Acceptance.*

Frail beings, tall and skinny. Lacking strength and muscle and work ethic. Being so close to one made Brokk sick and suddenly, he realized that the King had done his forefathers a great mercy by sending them to the Jark home world. The intermixing with other races had made them strong and sturdy, capable of waging warfare and defending their home world. The Tassians, by contrast, were pathetic and incapable, as if their only strategy was faith in the corporate protection by a bureaucratic and incompetent system of galactic government. "What does she do in your cabinet, Ebb?"

"I'll sign it," he said, exhaustedly. "I'll sign it."

Lago, who had been resting on his knuckles, startled at how quickly Ebb had folded his cards and hurriedly brought the charter to Ebb for signature.

Ebb stared at it for a minute as if he was reconsidering his offer, and Brokk pushed the female closer to the edge again. "Speak into it Ebb," he snarled.

Ebb drew in some air with his pointed nostrils and spoke the words inscribed at the bottom of the scroll. "Without coercion or threat of repercussion, I, Chancellor Roderik Ebb, dutifully sign this charter and agree our people will peacefully transition governance to the Jarks." He then placed his eye to the scroll, forever locking his words with his very soul, thus completing the signature. Lago stepped backward, but Brokk remained with the Tassian female at the edge of the building.

"I'm surprised you surrendered your people so easily," Brokk said, almost disappointed. "If someone took over my home, I would never give them power; no matter how many of my friends and family were slaughtered."

"That's the difference between us, Brokk," Ebb said defeated. "My people have value and I serve them for their good; my power in governance is worthless if I cannot ensure that good."

"I guess we have a different perspective on good," he retorted, jerking the woman toward the edge of the building. "But just so you know I'm not soft…" Brokk gave her a thrust, and the woman's screams abated after the same three seconds of freefall as the previous victim. Ebb fell to his knees as guards dragged him off of the roof and back down the stairs. Soon, it was just Lago that remained.

"Lago," Brokk said, looking down at the bodies and the crowd of panicked Tassians below. "I need the darkest curtains you can find for my new office and bedroom. Bring engineers down from our vessels and make this building as dark as our home world." Lago acknowledged, but Brokk stopped him from leaving with a wave of his hand while he still examined the street. "Give these orders to our commanders: Each man, woman, or child who protests these two deaths is to be executed publically by this evening. Round up all the men who are capable of fighting, use the archives to determine ages and training, and put them into internment camps. It's time to tighten our grip on this planet and its people." He returned his eyes to Lago to make his final point. "If the council decides to visit this place when they learn about our invasion, I don't want anyone alive who doesn't fear me enough to be terrified of the consequences for speaking to the council."

Lago departed, but Brokk remained on the roof. He closed his eyes and gazed upward toward the sun, letting it splash his face with its rays. *I hate that sun*, he thought, suddenly realizing he hated both suns equally.

Eventually, he left the rooftop for his office to transmit the signed charter to his government. Brokk had no interest in dealing with the galaxy or their laws. He would allow his planet's king to deal with the politics behind the invasion.

He was, however, excited to be able to report a completely stable planet so that the Jarks could begin plans for the pilgrimage. Brokk knew there was no way to defeat an actual insurgency should one arise, and he certainly couldn't change the norms of the Tassian culture. In fact, he expected that the Tassian people would always rise up so long as they were the majority. A mass colonization and a new generation of Jarks was the only thing that could truly conquer this planet and its people.

***

By the time Remmel's scouts returned, the sun's heat was already being felt along his lines. As a result, Remmel found himself dedicating an exhausting number of resources to purifying drinking water and searching for food simply to keep his army in fighting shape. Sweating and covered in mud, Jorte, the commander of his reconnaissance squadron, reported to his tent.

"What did you see out there?" Remmel asked, pulling up a chair and giving the commander a canteen full of cold water. Jorte took a swig, poured some over his white hair, and shook his head, sending droplets across the tent like a muddy dog coming in from the rain.

"There are way more Jarks on the ground than I had initially suspected, sir. My positions across the capital alone are reporting over a million Jark soldiers, and that's just the capital. They've set up robust checkpoints and roadblocks, and their fighters continually patrol the skies. Most people are staying in their homes, and some of the Jark propaganda suggests that they may be able to see some basic services coming back on soon like food fabrication, water, and electricity." Jorte paused to take another drink and smeared more water onto his face with his dirty hand. A smudged streak of dirt remained on his ruddy face, and when mixed with the water and sweat, began to bleed brown streaks down his cheeks and neck. "It's a hot one," he said, exhausted.

"Take your time, son." Remmel responded, gesturing for him to relax and take a breath.

Reaching into his deep green backpack, Jorte removed a sketch of the capital section of the city planet. "I've templated the Jarks' main defensive positions. You can see here, in red," he said, pointing to a red circle, "This is the capitol building and seemingly the main command center. I saw their leader personally execute two Tassian officials from the rooftop." Remmel examined the map, and Jorte waited patiently for the old commander to finish.

Finally, Remmel looked up, and Jorte continued. "Probably the last thing worth noting is that I've decided to pull my scouts from the city and instead set up positions just beyond the city's limits." This piqued Remmel's attention, but before he could ask why the young commander had deliberately disobeyed his orders, Jorte continued his explanation. "They've begun searching house to house for any men over the age of eighteen and are scanning entire city blocks for weapons. Worse yet, the men they find, they are rounding up and putting into camps."

He paused to take a breath, and Remmel knew he wasn't yet finished, but his hesitation indicated that there was still even worse yet to come.

"Apparently the camps are nothing more than laser wire out in the sun. But there are rumors," Jorte tacked on, "that those camps aren't just to isolate military-aged men but soon for women and children too. People are saying that the Jarks are torturing and killing them for any information on rebel forces."

Jorte fell silent as he completed his report and smeared another glob of sweaty dust from his forehead and onto his hand. Remmel looked away, first at the ground and then at the green canvas walls of his humble new office. He didn't want the young man to see his face reflect the visible fear that shook him from the last comment. Remmel had seen these camps before, and they only led to tragedy. Instantly, his mind went back to the pink-and-white river on the distant moon of another race's solar system. The river, the guilt, the anguish, the nightmares. Remmel felt it all and he felt it all continually.

"Sentient beings have always done wretched things to one another for no good reason," he finally responded to Jorte. "There is a wickedness that transcends us all." Remmel hesitated as he considered saying more but stopped short. He was always careful not to bring personal and private matters into his relationship with his subordinates. "Good report, Jorte," he said. "Give the Jarks a day to establish themselves. You were right to withdraw from the city. Once the Jarks clear a few blocks, infiltrate the city and begin telling our people that we are here, that we need food and water, and that we will be a refuge and a defense to all who want to come live among us. The internment camps won't stop with the men. Soon, it will be the women and the children too; you'll see."

Remmel dismissed his scout and remained seated for a while longer, reviewing the map and organizing his thoughts. He had hoped delegates from the galaxy would have come by now, but it appeared that the Tassians were going to be on their own. He would have to concentrate his forces and strike at the heart of the Jark command center. Only if he could succeed in destroying the leadership could this invasion be thwarted.

Remmel considered going outside but was suddenly gripped with despair. In that dark green tent that hid the sunlight from his body, Remmel allowed it to hide his sins as well. Those camps, those nasty camps that he tried so hard to forget. Remmel wasn't just a prisoner in one; he had escaped, but escape brought a price Remmel never thought he would have to pay.

As the candle flickered in his dark green tent, the old commander replayed the events of his terrible past. "The ends just don't justify the means," he said to himself quietly. "I wish I could take it back; I wish I could."

Remmel wasn't just speaking to himself. In his mind, Remmel was speaking to two other men, two other Tassian prisoners. One, too sick to climb from his prison bed couldn't defend himself when Remmel stole his extra food each day to gain strength for the escape. Each day, the man grew weaker and protested less. The night before Remmel fled the camp, the poor soul starved to death. "This would be worth it," a foolish young Remmel told himself. "If I don't get out, we all die. It's one life for all of us."

But it wasn't just one life. On that pink-and-white river Remmel found another Tassian who had escaped. As before, however, it was a competition for resources and a testament of will power. In the early morning, Remmel seized the man's rifle and beat him to death for making noise in his sleep. "We can't be found out," Remmel told himself at the time. "We can't be heard."

In that dark green tent, the old commander once again allowed himself to weep. *Men do wretched things to one another for no good reason*, he thought to himself. *For no good reason.*

CHAPTER THIRTEEN

Casika woke to a knock on her cabin door. Her head throbbed, and she suddenly realized that she had been lying face down in a puddle of her own drool. Groggily, she rolled to the side of the bed, pushed herself to her feet, and stumbled toward the door. It was Gemini waiting to escort her back to his office.

"How'd you sleep?" he asked cheerfully as he leaned in to get a closer look at her healing head injury. "Is it bothering you any?"

"Like a rock," she responded, allowing him to examine her. "What time is it anyway? I don't even remember falling asleep."

Gemini laughed. "It's past lunch. Why don't you throw on a new outfit and meet me down in the lobby in a few minutes? There are some spares in the closet that you can wear until you get a chance to make yourself something that you would typically wear at home."

Casika smiled and closed the door. Spinning around the room, she found the wardrobe and three gray coveralls that were loosely fitting and had zippers that ran from one foot, across the body, and secured at the neck. Casika hurriedly pulled a fresh uniform off the hanger, zipped herself up in it, ruffled her hair in the mirror, and raced out the door and down the stairs to meet Gemini.

Upon approaching the lobby, she saw him speaking with the pink-skinned Pisky from the night before. "Of course," she could hear him saying, "but these things take time, you know?"

"I...I...I'm very...v...very worried about the progress," the poor creature managed to stutter out. Casika instantly took pity on the small thing but couldn't help but giggle a bit as she approached. His tiny body was barely tall enough to reach Gemini's waist, and the two speaking to each other looked like something from a child's cartoon rather than real life.

Gemini, noticing Casika walk up, tried to cut the conversation short. "I have to go. I'll have my executive officer look into it again, OK?" The Pisky, clearly frustrated with his ability to communicate his distress to the Mateens, continued to speak, but Gemini held up a hand and silenced him. "I promise, we'll look into it. Why don't you find something good to read?" he asked, leading the man to the bookshelf in the corner.

Gemini returned to Casika and sighed. "Most of the people here are frustrated with the time it takes our government to process their paperwork, but the truth is, we don't know him from anyone else. It's important that we do our research before letting him live among our people."

"He doesn't look like he is much of a threat," Casika retorted out of pity for the man.

"Maybe. Maybe not. Even if he isn't a threat to a full-grown Mateen, what about to a Tassian? What about to another Pisky? Do you know how much strength you need to detonate a bomb? To propel a rider engine into a bus full of children? Do you…"

"All right, all right, already!" she blurted out. "You win." She paused to soak in his silence. "Goodness, give a girl a break," she joked.

Gemini chuckled. "Are you hungry?" he asked, turning to give her space to follow him.

"No thank you." Casika responded, patting her belly. "I'm not sure I'm ready to eat yet." Gemini gave her a suspicious glance, and she quickly changed the subject to avoid any additional medical testing. "These sure are nice rooms," she rushed, gesturing back to the stairwell and her quarters. "Do you always leave them vacant for guests?"

As they chatted, Gemini turned left and led her down the hallway back toward his office. "A starship has many functions, Casika. Even though this is my ship, it's no different." The two turned again and walked down a side corridor, passing a series of Mateen recruiting posters that were hanging along the interior wall. One poster showed a gray-faced Mateen soldier posing on the top of a cliff while a starship rose above him in the distance. Boldfaced words above the poster read, *Exporting Courage to Planets Everywhere.*

Gemini was still talking about his ship, and Casika suddenly realized that she hadn't heard a word he was saying. "Those guest rooms were initially built as officer's quarters for an infantry brigade traveling with us as part of a potential ground invasion. As the galaxy sunk into peace and the Galactic Council executed their duties, we have used them for distinguished guests and refugees while they wait for their clearances to be processed to live among our people."

Gemini turned left again, and Casika followed, looking out at the vacuum of space each time they passed a window. Space was still new to her and, despite the circumstances, she couldn't help but let her imagination run wild as she stared at the star-speckled void beyond. As they approached a large circular viewing station, however, the void was filling with countless asteroids. "Are we in an asteroid belt right now?"

"We are. Do you recognize it?" he asked, turning once again to face her.

In the distance, Casika could see two bright dots that appeared to be orbiting each other. "Tassi?" she exclaimed with glee. "Are we back at Tassi?" Her excitement, however, only lasted for a moment, and soon elation mixed with fear began to fill her facial features. "Why are we here?" she finally asked somberly. "Do you intend to return me?"

"Certainly not, Casika." Gemini responded reassuringly. "I offered you asylum on our planet, and the offer is still yours to claim or reject. We traveled here half an orbit ago." Gemini paused and looked out the window. To Casika, it seemed like he was trying to figure out how to phrase his next sentence.

"Just come out with it," she blurted. "I don't want to hear it with any filters."

Gemini returned his gaze to her, and his dark red eyes instantly seemed to penetrate deep into Casika's soul. Whenever he looked directly at her, she found herself regretting her previous rash speaking. As usual, his deep, calm voice relaxed her as soon as he began speaking.

"The Galactic Council has determined not to intervene in the invasion of your home world."

She gasped. "How can that be?" Casika was angry, and her face felt red hot as blood rushed to fill her cheeks. "Didn't they realize it was unprovoked? Don't they understand that we rely on the Galactic government for most of our defense?"

Gemini held her gaze and withered her anger until he was certain she was finished. "The council passed this matter to a cultural affairs office, which determined this to be an internal cultural matter between the Jarks and the Tassians. They claim to have spoken to the Jarkian government and have been assured of a takeover in full accordance with galactic law and where full services will be offered to the Tassian people so long as the new government is able to safely apply those services to each district. Allegedly, your chancellor has even signed the agreement and stepped down from power."

Casika didn't respond but shifted her gaze from his eyes to the asteroid belt beyond. A massively jagged rock drifted past the ship to block her view of the twin suns at the center of her system. "Why are we here?"

"The Mateens don't belong to the Galactic Council and have never relied on any outside group to guarantee our security," he responded. "We have our own interest in ensuring this isn't simply an imperialistic starting point for the Jarks…a theory that occupies the minds of many of my people."

"So, what are you doing?" she asked, allowing hope to rush back into her veins and restart her heart like a jolt of electricity into a dead battery.

"I'm watching. Looking for proof. Ensuring there is a just war being fought. Ensuring all of our people can continue in peace as the council has been led to believe."

Casika started to cry and turned away from the window. "They killed so many…" she wept, fighting back tears. "How can you watch for a 'just war'?" Without waiting for an answer, she turned and looked intensely at Gemini's crimson red eyes and held his gaze. "Will I ever be able to return home? What will be left of my people if I do?"

"I'm sorry, Casika," Gemini responded, placing his hand on her shoulder. "But I didn't bring you down here to look out a window."

Wiping the tears from her eyes, she fixated her gaze on a button on Gemini's uniform. Its bright bronze shine captivated her for a moment and provided an emotionally neutral place for her to stare. The button was safe. It was unchanging. In truth, it was a lot like Gemini, but it lacked the judgment that she suspected he held deep within him. It was just an object. Gemini wasn't, she hoped, just an object.

"I've been ordered to send a scouting party to your planet's surface." Her eyes shot back from the shiny bronze button and locked with his. "My scouts believe they have found a rebel commander hiding on the outskirts of the city; it's possible he is responsible for your people's resistance, their only resistance. I'd like you to accompany me."

She stared blankly for a moment, processing what he was telling her. *Return to Tassi. Return to the war.* "Why do you need me? I'm not a soldier or a diplomat—"

"But you are Tassian," he interrupted. "You can be our guide and our go-between. You can vouch for our intentions and our legitimacy. You can help us to establish trust in an otherwise shaky relationship. Most of all, you can hopefully help us to determine the truth. We don't know your people, we can't read their expressions, and we can't understand their phrases beyond the simple word-for-word translation."

Return to Tassi. "I was a nobody. I was a waitress…a vagrant. Nobody respected me. How much could I really help?"

"You'll never know how much help you can be to us and to your people unless you accompany me," he responded.

"Why are you pushing this?" Casika asked. "Why are you willing to go to war for my people?"

"My family and I were farmers. Whenever a fire started in the dry season on someone's farm, we all ran to help them put it out. Even though we were competing to sell crops and livestock, the risk of the fire spreading to other farms far outweighed the risk of honest competition. Your people deserve to be free, and right now, the Jarks feel a lot like fire. Have an escort take you to my quarters once you've made your decision. We will leave tomorrow if you want to come with us."

Gemini left Casika at the window and walked down the corridor toward his bridge. She watched him for a moment as he confidently strode down the hallway, greeting members of his crew as he passed them. *Return to Tassi*, Casika thought, once again fixing her eyes on the twin suns in the void of space. She would, of course, return to Tassi—

but not for Tassi's sake. It was Gemini who gave her the opportunity to thrive when Tassi was unable to. It was Gemini who offered her refuge and a new start on his home world when Tassi provided no such opportunity. It was Gemini whom she would swear her allegiance to, and she determined in that moment that she would accompany him anywhere. If he needed her, she was grateful for the chance to accompany him.

***

Shouting and gunfire tore Remmel out of his daily update meeting trance. Desperate for an excuse to end the brutal operations update that rarely fed him any useful information, he shot from his chair and ran outside. The young Tassian officer leading the brief stuttered at first, then continued, and then stopped altogether as he found himself alone in the drab green command tent with all other participants eager to follow their general from the briefing and into the potential battle.

"What's going on?" Remmel shouted, running toward the line where the shots had been fired.

"False alarm, sir," responded a young, sweaty-faced officer who ran to his side. "Refugees, we're processing refugees from the city," he panted. "They came up on one of our positions without identifying themselves and one of our soldiers fired a warning shot."

"C'mon! We've got to be better than this!" Remmel bellowed at the young man in frustration, sending him jumping backward and shielding his face from the inevitable slap that he believed would come next.

It didn't. Instead, Remmel grabbed the man by his collar and brought his face close to his own. "We identify before we shoot, and we don't shoot at our own people you fool!" Remmel released him by shoving him backward and continued moving quickly up a small hill toward the front line. Upon cresting the hill, he nearly fell backward at the sight. Hundreds, if not thousands, of people carrying children, food, baskets, blankets and more were being processed through the trench and into a holding area on the other side. Most were women, but there were men intermingled with the larger families and a large number of teenage boys as well. "Get the refugees further off the line," he ordered to some soldiers looking on. "And bring them food and water."

Remmel looked at Cale, who had arrived behind him. Cale wasn't responsible for their defense, but Remmel trusted him to look after a majority of the camp's operations.

"These people are scared, Dad," he told his father. "I spoke to a group of the older men that led them here. They said that the Jarks are going door to door. First, they were just taking men, but overnight, they shifted tactics and began loading up women and children too. People are saying they are simply executing them while others claim there is some sort of re-education going on."

"Executing them?" Remmel gasped. "Why would they..." he trailed off.

"I'll keep talking and get more information from our scouts," Cale responded. "I'd like to start training all the men who are capable of fighting." He paused. "I'd like to arm the women too."

"That's a good idea, son," the old commander responded. "We're going to need to be prepared for more refugees too. I've been considering finding a way to access the underground farms from here. Take your engineers and work on a solution for both. I'm going to find out what I can from those elders."

Cale gave him a brief smile before moving off to his left toward the refugees pooling at the base of the hill. Remmel watched his son for a moment longer and then shifted his gaze toward the trees. A steady flow of people continued to walk in a line out of the forest and toward his men. To Remmel, they looked scared, hungry, and desperate.

In systematic fashion, the guards at the trench patted each person down for weapons or radios that might signal a Tassian spy working for the Jarks. So far, it looked as if there were none. After a person was searched, he or she was ushered into a group. Men to one side and women with children on the other.

A third group consisted of teenagers of both genders. It was this group that Cale examined the most and spent the majority of his time. These were the real future of Tassi, and Cale was going to make sure that they fought for it.

CHAPTER FOURTEEN

"Ahh, I'm glad you could join me," Brokk said, leaning back in the chancellor's favorite wood and ivory chair, made from five-horned beasts that even the bravest hunters avoided if the bounty wasn't worth the risk. Set before the conqueror was a gourmet spread of crackers, cheese, meats, and wine, all displayed in Chancellor Ebb's personal crystal bowls meant to bathe the food in the glory of the twin suns above. Considering himself a modern visionary of the culinary arts, Ebb had believed that food became a delicacy when its colors not just shone, but exploded outward with such richness that one could taste the meal before it ever touched the lips.

At the center of the table was a single candle, tall and elegant, propped up by a crystal candelabra. The candle was surrounded by green half-moon wreaths made of Tassian pines, all placed atop a solid white table cloth. Two Tassian servants stood at the doorway with their heads bowed to the ground. Brokk would not allow the women to look at him as he enjoyed the food that they had prepared for their new master.

"I suppose I should be thanking you, Ebb," Brokk continued over the delicate sound of classical music in the background. "If you hadn't lived so elegantly, I wouldn't be able to enjoy any of this today." Brokk stood to greet his guest, not with a handshake, but with a gesture toward a chair across from him. "Where are my manners, Ebb? Please sit down and join me for a meal."

"I'm not hungry," Ebb responded. In truth, he was, but the thought of dining with such a monster turned the hunger pangs in his stomach into something else entirely.

"I insist," hissed Brokk. "It's customary to offer your adversary one final meal prior to his execution. I'm certain you will not want to miss yours. I am told the underworld has little to do with food." Brokk looked at the escorts who had led him in. "Seat him," he demanded.

"I'll seat myself," Ebb returned with a sudden flare of aggression. Brokk's threat of death wouldn't shake the old chancellor. He had steeled himself for the time that Brokk would execute him and he determined in his mind that it would be better to die than to watch the remainder of Brokk's cleansing helplessly from his prison cell.

The music that flowed from a small player in the corner was deep in tone and soothing. Ebb closed his eyes for a moment upon reaching his chair and allowed the keys from the musician's clavichord to drum into his mind. He had always loved keyed instruments and had amassed a collection of the finest classical works Tassi had produced.

"What do you think of the drapes?" Brokk asked. Ebb hadn't even noticed them; the room had simply appeared brighter than his prison cell below. But now that he looked around, he realized that the dull candle burning was the only light in the room. Brokk had completely covered the crystal windows and walls with thick black drapes. Tears filled Ebb's eyes as the symbolic nature of this act sunk in. Brokk's ceremonial blocking of the sun was more than just for comfort. He was blatantly demonstrating a new form and system of government to Ebb before his execution. This crystal capitol building was supposed to show the people that they could see all the way through their government whenever they wanted. The transparency of this office was no more; now it was replaced with a dark and oppressive regime, focused only inward, only on power and greed.

"I hate your planet. I hate the never-ending light. I hate the colors. I hate your people," Brokk said with a snarl. His golden skin was darkened in the candlelight and as the dim flame flickered back and forth, his sharp white teeth soon became the focus of Ebb's attention. Brokk was not a man, but a demon—a creature from another world sent here by some evil power to torment the Tassian people, to destroy their way of life and desecrate their religion. No, he was not a man. He was pure monster.

"You will never be able to hide from the light, Brokk." Ebb retorted defiantly. "You will never eradicate all of my people. Justice will come to our land. The Galactic Council…"

"The Galactic Council has approved our invasion!" Brokk gleefully shouted. He was like a child who had just stolen a toy. "I guess you missed the celebration from your cell, but they want nothing to do with Tassi. It's ours now."

Ebb couldn't tell if Brokk was telling the truth or lying. *Is this some tactic to convince me to concede more, or is it simply the outpouring of his vanity to celebrate this tiny victory?*

"Why are you so happy if you hate this place?" Ebb asked. He truly wanted to know but believed it had more to do with having it than it did enjoying it. Brokk was just like a child who had stolen a toy. The child would never want to play with the thing; it was only a matter of keeping it away from anyone else.

"Because it should have been ours all along, Ebb." Brokk looked down at the doomed man's plate. He hadn't touched a thing. "I suppose you really aren't hungry, eh?" he asked one last time.

Ebb didn't respond, and Brokk rose to his feet and moved toward the black canvas that covered the large window overlooking the city. "In truth, I don't really enjoy your company, Ebb. If you are going to refuse your final meal, I won't waste my evening with you. We've gathered up your people to witness this. I want you to know that I don't plan to let them live much longer than you, but it's important that they see their leader fall. People should see the end of their government and the beginning of a new one, even if those people won't be around to watch it fully ushered in."

Brokk lifted his arm and pulled the heavy drapery over to expose the window. Two guards picked the poor chancellor up from his chair and brought him to the crystal opening that Brokk had pushed outward. A breeze rushed into the sealed-off building and with it came the scent of Tassi that Ebb had come to love. He could smell the sharp salt of the sea and the rich evergreen forests all in one.

Looking down, Ebb could see his people. Before him was a massive crowd in the square below, surrounded by soldiers clad in black, forced to watch his humiliating execution. "I won't make you endure the fall like I've done to the others," Brokk said in a way that asked for a thank you, as if this was some glorious gift of mercy and grace he was imparting on his foe. "Do you have anything at all that you'd like to say? This might be the very last time you ever get to speak," he taunted, removing a dagger from his belt.

"You're wrong about everything. There will be justice for you," Ebb said. As soon as he uttered those final words, he felt an intense pain in his abdomen where Brokk drove the silver blade into his flesh. He did not scream. He wouldn't give Brokk that pleasure, but his strength failed him, and, staggering for a moment, he reached out his hand to steady himself on something. Anything. Brokk caught it and locked eyes with him for just a second. In the pure light from above, Ebb saw only evil in the man's expression. Then he was weightless. Brokk had lied. He did let him count the seconds to the bottom.

CHAPTER FIFTEEN

As Gemini's fleet drifted silently in the Tassian asteroid belt, Gemini and a party of fourteen men boarded a small shuttle prepared for a journey to the planet's surface. With the group, which consisted of Gemini's personal security detachment, was Casika, dressed in the same brown-and-green camouflage that had been specially crafted to match the lush foliage on the planet's surface. As with each planetary deployment, weapons, clothes, and equipment were all custom built to ensure maximum survivability and effectiveness.

While not a ground soldier, to be a Mateen fleet commander Gemini was required to serve as an infantryman or scout during a period of his career. Gemini chose to be a scout and over a three-year period served in several key battles with other planetary members of the newly forming Galactic Order. Gemini cherished this experience, not for the fighting, but for the knowledge that he had acquired. Simply put, Gemini never knew how intelligent one had to be to outmaneuver the enemy in a complex land war.

The soldiers with him who now made up his personal security detachment were men he had hand selected from throughout his career. These men had been put through rigorous testing and were forced to apply ground combat skills in a variety of complex environments. Gemini felt strongly that the group going to the planet's surface with him were battle-tested warriors and more than capable of protecting their beloved space commander than any other warrior in the galaxy.

As she found her seat on the shuttle, Casika peered forward to see Gemini going over a digital map of their landing zone. He carried a green-and-brown assault rifle strapped across his lap and a multitude of gadgets that hung from his armored chest. His dark gray face was covered with a thin mesh veil, but his deep red eyes shone through the darkness and seemed to burn into her soul as long as she held his gaze. Interrupting her, a large Mateen warrior approached her canvas-strapped seat and began checking that she was properly secured for the flight.

"Nervous?" he asked through the universal translator embedded in her ear.

She returned a faint smile and acknowledged that she was. Nervous actually was an understatement; she was terrified.

"Don't worry about a thing," he quickly responded. "My name is Arden, and I've been assigned to keep watch over you while we're down there." Arden kneeled down next to her and pointed at a thin glass panel that was sewn into her uniform at her forearm. "This is your control center for the uniform we've built for you."

Reaching up, he grabbed the same thin veil that Gemini had on his uniform and rolled it down over her head, attaching it to her camouflage jacket at the magnetic buttons on her shoulders. Her vision dimmed a little in the faint red light of the shuttle, but generally she found herself able to see extremely well.

"This is your cloaking device and heads-up display," he told her. "When we land on the surface, we are all going to initiate our cloaks so we can move to the rebel camp undetected. In addition to cloaking your face, this veil will show you our locations so we aren't invisible to one another, as well as perform some intuitively helpful functions like providing you with places to find cover if we are getting shot at or showing you strengths and weaknesses of an enemy target. You'll get the hang of it after only a few steps."

"What will you look like through the veil?" she asked.

"You'll see our shadows, like gray outlines. As soon as you lift the veil, we won't be visible, so make sure to close it and maintain your heads-up display at all times." Arden finished strapping Casika in and stepped back to his seat. Casika fiddled a bit more with her veil and looked up to see Gemini standing over her.

"When we get to the planet, we will lead you to the camp," he said. "We'll walk through their camp like ghosts in the night until we find the commander's tent. Remember, your role is to make him feel comfortable and convince him that we mean no harm. That means that you'll be the one to unveil first on my signal, then the rest of us will follow."

Casika nodded and suddenly realized that she wasn't just nervous or terrified. She was petrified. The weight of an actual military mission rested heavily on her shoulders, and she rapidly thought through all the things that could go wrong—that should go wrong. They could crash, be detected, be fired at by the Tassians who wouldn't realize that they were there to help, or worse yet, be captured by the Jarks.

Gemini rechecked her seat restraints and took her hand in his. "We're going to be OK," he said warmly. She wondered if she had looked as frantic as she felt but was glad to have his warm, stony hand secured around hers. Wishing his hand would remain, she was disappointed when he departed and returned to his own chair, taking with him the brief comfort that he had generously offered up.

The engines of the shuttle whirred to life and vibrated her muscles against her bones and her cheeks against her teeth. The dim red light that filled the cabin flickered and then turned off as the craft lurched forward out of its resting place in the hangar and drifted out into open space. This would mark the first time that Casika had ever willingly flown in space. She considered both of her previous experiences to be under duress and therefore unable to be considered true space flights.

Unlike the noisy transport shuttle that she had used to escape from Tassi, this one was almost completely silent. The whining of its engines abated as soon as they left the hangar and now it felt as if they were floating aimlessly without power, simply waiting for the craft to eventually be sucked into some planet's gravity and crash, just like Casika's previous trip. Her heart raced as she reconsidered the crash and fought desperately to beat back the scourge of memories from just a few days ago.

Her logical self knew that they weren't simply drifting, and she took comfort it seeing the Mateen warriors sitting calmly without so much as flinching on all sides. Further abating her panic was the light from the dual-starred system suddenly shining brightly through the shuttle's windows. Yes, she thought, they were moving, and everything would be OK. Soon, very soon, Casika would be home.

How they evaded detection, she did not know. If asked how long she remained in that shuttle, she could not say. She only knew that suddenly she believed in a god she never believed in, and she prayed continuously during their voyage. When she finally saw the familiar trees of her city's outskirts, Casika was not simply relieved, but was overwhelmed with emotion.

From the moment that they left the hangar until now, not a sound could be heard from their silent vessel as it swam through the black void of space. Suddenly, however, the mechanical noise of feet being deployed from the bottom of the craft hummed beneath her. Gemini disconnected his harness and rose to his feet along with his fourteen warriors, and then they simply disappeared from her sight.

Casika hurriedly fumbled with her harness as a door on the back of the shuttle opened to reveal the marshy outskirts of her homeland. She couldn't see anyone leaving the ship but fumbled all the more, panicked that she was being left behind. Just when she had given up almost all hope, a hand reached down to her forearm and turned on her computer. It was Arden's, and suddenly, the light gray shadows of Gemini and his warriors appeared outside the craft. Arden removed Casika from her seat, as if he was pulling a child from a carriage, and escorted her out into the Tassian sunlight that bathed her planet's surface. She was finally home. All the anxiety she had felt during the trip simply vanished as she let her face soak in the gentle rays of the sun. *Home.*

Birds chirped and insects hummed. Technically, it was dusk on her planet, which meant the two suns emitted an orange glow in the sky, but it never got too dark to see. She hadn't realized how much she had missed the cool breeze coming off of the ocean, carrying with it the scent of salt and memories of hundreds of childhood vacations. Vacations spent playing in the surf with her sisters and laying on the beach hours after the rest of the families had gone home.

Single file, the Mateen warriors and the lone survivor pushed through grass and shrubs as they moved deeper into the marsh. The entire movement was silent with the exception of an occasional breaking twig or the heavy breathing of Arden, who remained faithfully behind Casika at all times. Biting insects swarmed her as her feet sunk deep into the muck of the swamp, but they found no way into her suit.

Finally, Casika stopped and kneeled in the thick brush, letting the cool water from the marsh soak into her cloth pants and stain her previously immaculate garment. Ahead, she could see what looked like a clearing. Intuiting that she intended to look into the distance, her veil magnified her vision and she could suddenly see men behind machine guns while others dug trenches. Her veil, ever helpful, outlined the men in red, indicating that the computer had identified a potential threat. Data began streaming down her vision, indicating the models of weapons they carried, but to Casika the data meant nothing. This was the rebel headquarters. They had arrived.

A shadow moved toward her position along their thin line and whispered in her ear. It was Gemini. "We've found a hole in their lines. We are going to move very quietly into the trench and then out the other side." Gemini placed a hand on her shoulder to move her body to see where he was pointing. Then, he moved his hand toward a large green tent that had been covered with shrubs. "That's where we are going," he whispered.

Her veil, intuitive as ever, captured the movement and the gestures that Gemini made and marked the objects, as well as the path that they were to take to their final destination. It looked arduous, sometimes taking them within just a few meters of a rebel position, but she had an advantage. She was invisible.

She nodded and Gemini moved back toward the front of the line. The experience felt so entirely surreal that she had let fear take a backseat to the novelty and thrill of this experience. Now, however, as she found herself faced with infiltrating her own people's camp, fear crept back into the forefront of her mind and all the insecurities that came with it. She was nobody on Tassi, a vagrant with no prospects for a future and an outcast within her own society. *Could I really do what Gemini is asking? Will they listen to me and heed my advice?*

In all honesty, she should have been dead during the invasion, and, if not dead, captured and forced to wait on the tables of her people's enemy. As she watched the rebel camp from the thicket, she realized that not only would she have served their enemy, but if they paid better, she would have served them happily. She had no real concept of pride or nationalism. Tassi had merely taken from her. Everything had changed now, and she even felt new disgust for herself as she reflected on her past and how she had only been thinking of her own needs and not the greater good.

How could Casika possibly help Gemini? He was smart; surely he knew how little she was worth. Why did he bring her along?

Casika looked toward the city as it reflected the radiant oranges and reds of the two suns off of its magnificent crystal structures. All of the buildings reflected that light except the one in the center. The king's palace. Perplexed, she focused her gaze on it until her veil once again magnified her stare. Casika struggled to breathe at the sight of the majestic city's centerpiece. The once-shining tower was completely black, as if a dark magician's cloak had been simply draped over it. Without a chance to truly process what she was seeing, Arden tapped her on the shoulder. "We're moving again," he whispered.

***

By the time Remmel finished speaking with the elder refugees and comparing their version of the events with that of his intelligence officers, the sky was at its deepest orange of the night. Thin red clouds stretched across the horizon while the burnt orange sky cast an eerie and ominous glow into the opening of the tent. With night came the howls of creatures living in the swamp that Remmel had only heard about during soldiers' tales told around firesides. Because the soldiers were desperate for entertainment, the stories would swirl around camp in a frenzy. Remmel rarely believed them, but understood their purpose—to keep young men awake while on the midnight guard shifts. Still, the howls of predators continued to ring out in the distance, and on this particular night, he couldn't help but feel that he was being watched.

Remmel entered his tent and zipped it up behind him. Although no light entered the completely blackened tent, he knew precisely where to find the switch. Once the light was turned on, the walls and ceiling would spring forth in a soft glow to illuminate his work. The light, built specifically to save power in a field environment, was the result of bacteria that had been trapped in the canvas and stored the sun's energy for the night. All the switch would do is close the circuit and enable the bacteria to power the tent. As he reached to his left, however, Remmel found not a switch but a hand.

Before his brain allowed him the quarter of a second required to react to his intruder, the large hand of an even larger man smothered his mouth and drove him hard to the ground. His ribs hit hard against the canvas floor and the impact ripped his breath way. The man pressed his heavy body on top of Remmel, refusing to allow him to take another breath in. His desperate struggle only increased the weight on his body until he believed he would pass out. Just then, the pressure abated and a female voice whispered into his ear. "We aren't here to hurt you. If you remain quiet and do not scream for help, we will let you up to speak with us." Without another option, Remmel nodded, certain that although he could see nothing in the darkness, his attackers could see everything.

Suddenly, the lights hummed on and the gentle white glow from the canvas beamed all around him. Above him kneeled a young Tassian female, clothed in the camouflage of a foreign army. Although his attacker still covered his mouth, Remmel felt better seeing one of his own people.

"I promise we are here to help you, but the people I am with need your assurances before they reveal themselves. Do you promise to remain quiet?" she asked again.

Remmel nodded, and the hand slipped off his mouth, allowing him to speak. "I promise," he said. Instantly, the pressure came off of his back, and he was lifted to his feet. In the midst of the tent, the space in front of his eyes swirled and vibrated as if sound waves had suddenly become visible to the naked eye; three camouflaged soldiers removed their cloaks. They were Mateens.

The Tassian female spoke to him again in the form of an introduction. "Please," she said, "listen to the people I have brought with me. They rescued me during this invasion and want to help." The woman then stepped aside and a large Mateen male stepped into her place. He smiled and reached out his hand.

"Please forgive our security measures," he said. "I'm sure you understand our precautions in the midst of such uncertainty. I want to make absolutely clear our desire to aid your cause. I'm Gemini, a fleet commander of one of many Mateen space fleets."

Rattled but composed, Remmel took his outstretched hand and shook it. "Remmel," he responded, neglecting to give his rank and position within the army. "What brings you to my tent, Gemini?"

"A few days ago, we picked up Casika," he said gesturing to the Tassian. "She was the lone survivor of a shuttle that had been attacked by a Jark warship; we've been trying to understand this invasion ever since."

"I can assure you, Gemini, it was unprovoked," he responded, motioning for Gemini to take a seat at his field desk. "And I'm grateful for the aid you provided to one of our people."

"What's their interest in Tassi?" Gemini asked, accepting the commander's offer.

Remmel moved around to his side of the desk and felt his ribs with his left hand as he took his own seat. "Who is the ape you had laying on top of me?" he asked, shifting topics for the sake of humor. Gemini gave a brief smile but didn't offer any retort or apology. Instead, Remmel found himself being studied by the stony-faced monster. His red eyes probed deeply into the old commander's mind, but Remmel wasn't alarmed. He had served long ago with the Mateens and found them to be sturdy and honorable. As they sat in his tent today, Remmel believed that he could trust their intentions even if they were potentially self-serving.

Still, although a historical relationship existed between the two planets, Remmel and the Tassians had long been abandoned by the Galactic Order, a fact that took an enemy invasion for his government to realize, and the relationship with the Mateens had dried up even before that. He knew he couldn't truly count on the Mateens beyond their own interests and wasn't sure he was ready to answer the fleet commander's questions. If the Mateens had been sent here out of mutual concern, he would accept their help, but not without suspicion.

"I should ask you the same question," Remmel responded at last. "What is anyone's interest in Tassi? And you," he said, turning toward Casika, "how did you find yourself so lucky as to be rescued by the Mateen commander?"

Casika began to speak, but was stifled by Gemini's hand, which shot up from his lap nearly as soon as the question was asked. "She is a refugee of this war, crashed on one of our moons. We've provided her medical aid and a safe place to stay. That's all you need to know about her. As for me," Gemini continued, "my interest in Tassi is completely self-seeking," he responded flatly.

Remmel was taken aback by this honesty, but before he could respond, Gemini continued.

"But I don't think you have even the smallest capability to judge me for that, given your current situation. You'll simply have to trust that our interest in stability is mutually beneficial and that after our work here is done, neither of our governments will be indebted to the other."

Remmel pondered for a moment but finally conceded. There would be no extra benefit he would be able to hold over the fleet commander's head and no way of knowing what the Mateens planned to do post-invasion. Still, it was better to have an isolationist like the Mateens in his corner rather than a group of imperialists like the Jarks. "I believe the Jarks have come to take over my planet, eradicate my people, and establish Tassi as their new capital," he said at last.

"Impossible," Gemini responded, his crimson eyes staring into Remmel's own.

The old commander, however, refused to look away. "In the last six hours, our camp has taken thousands of refugees all reporting the same thing. Jark soldiers are rounding them up and executing civilians in the streets. The ones they don't execute, they send to camps, and only God knows what they are doing to them there. These aren't soldiers or combatants—they are civilians. Worse yet, I just received another disturbing report that our chancellor was thrown from the same building. If they are executing the leaders of our government, the Jarks must know that Tassi is now theirs for the taking. If not ownership, what other purpose could this invasion have?"

Gemini's expression flattened once more, and his eyes flickered from a deep red to a golden bronze and back again. The change was so faint, Remmel almost didn't catch it, but he had seen it before and knew what was happening. In that very moment the Mateen collective was discussing his fate, comparing the facts, and determining their next move. Remmel waited until Gemini's eyes flickered once more, allowing expression to return to the goliath's face.

"How long until you are ready for a counterattack?" Gemini asked.

"I'm ready now, but we cannot hold the capitol block for long. They've decimated our fleet, and my scouts have reported at least ten million Jark soldiers across the planet. I have a mere forty thousand, Gemini. It's possible that there are other garrisons that survived, but I don't know of any. Rounding them up will take time."

"I wish your estimates were accurate, Remmel, but we believe their numbers across this planet to be more like twenty million." He smiled as the number soaked in. "But your people still outnumber them by one hundred times. All they need is the courage and someone to synchronize a rebellion. What about refugees?"

"We're training them, yes. But they won't be ready…"

"To guard static positions?" Gemini challenged. "Surely you have some men and women who can simply point down a road and shoot."

Remmel sighed but conceded. He understood Gemini's urgency, and it was not just for Gemini. It was his people who were being executed in cold blood, and they deserved a hasty response if able. "When do you need us to be ready?"

Suddenly, a fourth Mateen warrior decloaked inside the tent behind Gemini. "This is Arden. He'll remain with you and help prepare your men to seize the capitol building. I believe we need to cut off the head to watch the warriors fall. He'll also provide a more detailed timeline once we have it. It's essential that we capture Brokk and force him to appear before the Galactic Council. Therefore, our attack must both isolate his headquarters as well as destroy his fleet to prevent escape. I believe that if we seize the capitol and capture their leader, the remaining soldiers will surrender or flee in the face of a full out rebellion."

"We'll be as ready as we can be," Remmel insisted, acknowledging Arden with a nod.

"One last thing," Gemini said, pressing his finger down on Remmel's desk. "This has to be a complete rebellion across all the provinces of Tassi. You must send your scouts to pass word among your people. Tell them to arm themselves, because in no more than three days they will be liberating their planet."

Remmel nodded again, and Gemini rose from his chair and pulled his cloak back over his head. Suddenly, the Tassian female disappeared along with the Mateen commander and his entourage. All that remained was Arden, a statuesque figure, darkened by the dim light glowing off the green canvas walls. Remmel remained at his desk as a gentle breeze pushed its way through the entrance, allowing himself to ponder his new alliance. In spite of this immense burden, Remmel allowed hope to creep into his heart. Even an ally as secretive as the Mateens could help save his people. He would do whatever was necessary to keep this new alliance strong, and suddenly, he was not only hopeful, he was grateful.

CHAPTER SIXTEEN

The loneliness of space was a topic that had been written about and studied by thousands of psychologists across the galaxy. Solutions included medications, virtual reality, three dimensional family rendering, dream machines, and a slew of other expensive gadgets; none of them helped. Sure, they masked the symptoms for a while, but they never cured the disease. Whether it burdened the sole person on a tiny vessel or the commander on a ship of thousands, the loneliness experienced was often too much to bear.

Lago stared motionless out of the window of his juggernaut-class battleship and pondered the blackness beyond. He had a different theory about loneliness, one perhaps that he would share with Jark psychologists once he was old and retired. Lago suspected that loneliness resulted in some intangible part of a person being taken from them during wormhole travel. He believed that when bodies became immaterial particles hurtling through the wormhole, the intangible stuff that made them who they were would get siphoned away—and with each jump, a little more of that intangible would leap away too.

He remembered his first jump and how excited the crew was to leap into battle behind Commander Brokk, but after the battle was over and the Jarks had won their prize, a feeling of loneliness had crept in. All of them felt it, as if space itself had seeped through their windows and pulled part of their very being into the void. Some of the men actually went crazy after that battle, but others, including Lago, were just different—just missing something.

Lago looked up at a silver disc that hung discretely on his far wall. The face of the disk was a dark gray, indicating that night had fallen on the planet. Because time was so hard to tell in space, a colored clock technique was used to tell the time of the planet currently being orbited. Dark gray meant dusk, and because this planet never had a night, the disk would never get any darker. During the day, the disc would become nearly white.

This method was used by most space crews and ensured that ship personnel were synchronized to the time of day that the ground forces were operating in. To help maintain a crew grounded in reality, the ship was also outfitted with sensors that dimmed lights, reactive walls that deepened their colors at the coming of night, and even artificial skies within private sleeping quarters.

For Lago, the very thought of nightfall only drove the loneliness deeper into his body, pressing at his very heart like needles in a pincushion. It was at these times that he wished he had never joined the fleet. Lago brought up his personnel log on a virtual computer terminal and counted the number of interstellar jumps he had made since joining. Four hundred and twenty-three.

According to his own calculations, Lago had only seventy-seven left until space will have taken everything from him. After that, he suspected he would be a mere shell, searching for the being that he once was without the knowledge to discern where he should even begin look. It was hopeless, of course, but everyone knew that. In a lot of ways, being a part of a star fleet was similar to rolling a piece of paper full of the solidified sulfuric mercury ooze on his home world and then smoking it. Everyone knew it was a habit that led to death, but few people ever stopped using the drug.

In these times of deep depression, Lago did his best to focus on the good—and right now the only good he could think of was that he was not on Tassi's surface. It wasn't the light that bothered him, although he much preferred the deep red sky of Jark, nor was it the war. He had fought many times and killed plenty of people. Lago even considered himself deaf to the cries of his opponents on the field of battle and enjoyed the opportunity to test his metal time and again.

It wasn't the occupation that bothered him, either. Carnage on the battlefield was a noble act. Two warriors fighting for the ultimate prize—the right to live another day. Jark occupation, however, was not noble. It was slaughter, a massacre, pure butchery. He knew its purpose and he even agreed with it…in part. But it wasn't noble. At the risk of sounding insubordinate, Lago always asked to depart Brokk's presence during the occupation phase of a battle. He suspected that Brokk knew, and he was grateful their friendship surpassed Brokk's ego;

Brokk always granted his request. And so Lago sat. Night after night he simply waited for the opportunity to meet one more foe on the battlefield, to execute one more jump through a wormhole, and to pick up the pieces of his soul once the fabric of space had ripped it away from him.

Unfortunately, Lago suspected that tonight would not be a night when he would feel the surge of adrenaline and meet his enemy on honorable ground. Tonight would be quiet, perhaps too quiet, and eventually he would fall asleep in his chair, staring out of his viewing window into the depths of space, while secretly searching inside his soul for the chunks that he believed to be floating beyond the pane.

CHAPTER SEVENTEEN

War. The three letter word rolled back and forth in Casika's mind during the silent trek toward the shuttle. She had escaped her planet once before in the midst of the initial invasion, and returning to it with the prospect of leaving again left a bittersweet taste in her mouth. On the one hand, she was eager to return again with Gemini, but on the other, deep within she knew that she could contribute more to the cause on her own planet, with her own people. Casika had seen extreme sorrow on the faces of so many of her people, all who had been forced from their homes and were living like rats while hiding from their enemy. When she escaped, she was afraid for herself, but now, at the prospect of leaving, she feared for her people.

As the group of warriors pressed silently through the brush, Casika stepped out of the column and paused to look back. In the cool of the evening, she gazed wearily toward the camouflaged camp that had been expanded to take in thousands of refugees. There were sick, hungry, and weary people who needed help; perhaps she could finally find a place within this group of people where she could contribute—where she would be needed.

"No one will blame you if you want to stay," Gemini whispered softly into her ear, as if reading her mind.

She didn't want to stay. She wanted to leave, she wanted to flee, she wanted to be a part of Gemini's crew, but she couldn't. She felt an inexplicable pull to stay with her people. "I want to stay with you, Gemini," she whispered back, aware that it was absurd for her to desire to be with a group of people that she had just met and saddened by what she inevitably was going to say next.

Gemini didn't let her add anything to her previous sentence. Removing his hood and taking her hand, he ended their conversation and crushed a portion of her heart that she hadn't even known existed. "You belong with your people," he said.

The stony-faced man disappeared again before her eyes. She hated him for saying that. She hated him for ending the conversation before she could offer a rebuttal. Any rebuttal. She hated him, but at the same time she knew that he said it for her, and so she hated him yet adored him all the more. She didn't know if she was alone, but after some time of silence and reflection, Casika began walking back toward the camp, her camp, and her people. The night was as dark as it had ever been, and lights that typically shone from the city and illuminated even the farthest swamps were dampened from the cloak of evil that had descended upon her once-peaceful planet.

As Casika walked, she felt a deep sense of peace penetrate into her very core. Casika was not going to be a victim of circumstances any longer. This war was giving her a chance to rebuild herself in a new image and to create a society focused on what people could do, not who they were. This very night, Casika felt like a new person, not one tossed by the wave of circumstance like a ship in the sea. She was a new person now, a strong person. She was reborn.

***

The cloak had helped, but Brokk had found something even better than a cloak to mask their building from the painful rays of the everlasting sunlight. The once-clear blue water in a crystal walled pool deep beneath his office, one that the weak Tassian race had used to rinse their filthy bodies, had been fully drained and replaced with the tools needed to convert not just the tower, but the entire city into a Jarkian masterpiece.

Priests dressed in their familiar golden cloaks stirred the silver mercury gently and hummed that same sweet tune that Brokk had become so accustomed to hearing before a battle. They said nothing; no priest ever spoke. Their language was for the dead. In a ritual that may seem even more barbaric than infant sacrifice, those children that were selected to become priests had their tongues and eyes removed and were thrust into training and service by the time they reached the age of four. A priest's vision was for the underworld, his speech for the dead. There was no need for the priest to see the things on the side of the living—he must forever focus on what lay beyond. Only the ears of the priest remained intact so that he could hear the orders of the

Jarkian ruling party and convey those orders to those beyond the grave.

As he watched from forty stories above in his dark crystal palace, Brokk found himself wondering if the dead would come and occupy their new home. *Could spirits travel halfway across the galaxy? Could they escape their fiery tomb on his home world and take up a new home on Tassi? Would they want to?*

As he pondered, the water began to bubble while the priests continued their familiar chant. Yes. They would come, and with them, Brokk would unleash a beast the Tassians had never seen. He would bring a glorious dark shroud over their land, a beast discovered in the distant corner of a worthless galaxy and only replicated by Jarkian science and necromancy deep within their mercury swamps. He would bring the grootslang.

CHAPTER EIGHTEEN

The path of war was always muddied and rarely the result of one man or action. For Gemini to blame Brokk outright for placing them on a path that would lead the two governments toward bloody conflict would be unfair; still he couldn't help but swell in anger toward the selfish commander for being so brutal toward the Tassian people. During his tour on the planet below, Gemini saw a degree of brutality he had never before witnessed. This was not a just war being fought against combatants, but a massacre of the entire Tassian home world.

By the time Gemini returned to his ship, his government had deliberated and made a decision. If such brutality could still exist in the galaxy, despite a Galactic Order whose job was to intervene before these types of things happened, then evil must be extinguished by other means. His own home had to be protected. They couldn't risk a new imperialistic power in their backyard, especially if it was allowed to gain strength and resources by conquering a new planet.

The Mateens had decided they would go to war, and Gemini's battle group would lead the charge. Messages from his government had already been sent to the Order seeking allies in their war but were rejected by all eight worlds that had seats on the Council for Galactic Peace and Security. The Council's response was laughable. Despite the eye-witness testimony that the Mateens invoked during the meeting with the Council, nothing could sway their opinion.

Gemini believed it was fear that motivated their indecision. In the face of war, the Council chose to condemn any aggressive Mateen action rather than to aid their cause. This infuriated Gemini more than the scoundrel of a man executing the innocent below and reinforced to him more than ever why his people remained isolated from the rest of the galaxy. He could trust no one but blood to come to his aid. Blood and self-interest of course.

Gemini ascended to the bridge in a silver pod-shaped elevator and erupted through the doors as soon as it arrived at his destination. "Castor," he said, taking his seat above his officers, "what's the status of our fleet?"

Castor spun around to greet his warrior captain. "Welcome back, sir," he said as he pulled up a holographic image of the asteroid belt that they had disguised themselves within. As Castor began the brief, holographic pilots from his battle group appeared around the walls of the circular bridge and prepared to watch and then provide Gemini a conditions check of their own forces. "We are here," Castor continued, pressing his finger into the asteroid belt to reveal Gemini's fleet. "As you can see, we are on the far side of the fifth planet as it orbits the dual suns."

Castor made a swiping motion with his hands and spun the hologram to show a top-down view from the perspective of his own ship. Four planets rotated inside the asteroid belt that engulfed the system. Within the rings of the planets were the two suns and a small planet between the two suns orbiting the larger of the two. It was the Tassian home world. As their view hovered, Castor manipulated the graphic to reveal the enemy defensive positions, sensors, and finally, their core armada. "As you can see, we have quite a distance to cover between their sensor range and our objective, but there really is only one main objective. Because of how quickly we've responded to this invasion, Brokk and his fleet have yet to truly establish themselves on the second planet beyond the two suns. Essentially, we have a singular objective with many small pieces all centered around the main planet Tassi."

Gemini remained silent as he analyzed the battlefield. The distance was large but not insurmountable. They would have to rely upon a withering amount of firepower to force the enemy armada to remain in their battle positions behind moons and within the magnetic pull of planets. He would also have to feign an assault against the enemy flank to force them to react to the fake enemy and mitigate the amount of firepower that they could concentrate forward.

The maneuver was risky, but as Gemini considered his enemy, he suspected he could tow asteroids from their orbit using his maintenance ships and force them on a course toward the main enemy armada. Towing a fleet of six asteroids would give the impression of an enemy battle group without having to commit his forces away from the main attack. The tows themselves would provide enemy radar a heat, life support, and weapon signature that should be sufficient to fool Brokk's fleet. Even more, if they managed to land additional throwaway thrusters on the asteroids themselves, it should be very convincing.

Castor saw his thoughts and began annotating them on the map using large sweeping arrows to distinguish a feint attack from the real one.

"What about the artillery?" Gemini asked. "We can't afford an interstellar barrage."

"We've located their position a few light years from here," his intelligence officer responded. "With your approval, we can disrupt their operations by initiating a counterfire."

"No. We might actually have a chance to examine and steal their technology. Jark artillery is the best in the galaxy, and the ability for munitions themselves to create wormholes has yet to be developed elsewhere. I want it. I want to capture their pieces and tow them back."

Castor remained silent, and Gemini knew that he didn't agree. "That's risky," he finally said.

"It's worth it," Gemini shot back. "Our men are well trained. Inform a commando team and synchronize the snatch to be a few hours before our feint assault. A loss of communications with the guns followed by a formation of ships coming from the asteroid belt should sufficiently divert their attention from our main assault. We only need one gun; have the commandos destroy the remainder in place." Gemini paused to examine the rest of the map while his crew waited for his final guidance. "What is our timeline?"

"Arden reports that rebel ground forces will be ready within the day. Incorporating your new guidance, Commandos will assault the interstellar artillery in T minus twenty hours, maintenance craft will initiate towing at T minus twenty-three hours, and your fleet will depart the asteroid field for the final assault in T minus twenty-six hours."

"Good. Any news from Arden about Casika?" Gemini wondered out loud.

"None," Castor responded.

"Fine. Finalize the order," Gemini said, standing to his feet. "I want commanders to brief me their understanding of the plan in twelve hours."

CHAPTER NINETEEN

Covered in grime, two women emerged from a line of trees that helped hide their camp from the city. Like so many others, these too followed the hidden clues that would bring them into the safety of Remmel's camp and under the security of the last warriors of Tassi. After being searched and questioned, the guards allowed the weary travelers to pass through their lines and join countless other refugees at the rear of the camp. Scouts would then retrace the route that the refugees took, searching for any enemy who may have followed the desperate travelers to their final location.

The portion of the camp dedicated to the exiles was ugly but sufficient. A well to supply water had been dug in the center of the dusty encampment, which was surrounded by huts of mud and piles of trash. Women were separated from the men, and each member was assigned a role. It was Casika's job to interview the refugees and find suitable places for them in the camp.

Men were easy. If you were able, meaning without disability, you were sent to weapons and tactics training as soon as you had been nourished. The well-bodied women were also sent to weapons training, assuming they did not have to care for young children. Here, there was no room for gender-specific tasks; all would either fight or provide support to those who could.

"We're going to take back the capitol in a few days," Casika told the latest survivors. "Can you shoot a weapon?"

The weary middle-aged women looked back at her blankly as they cupped bowls of hot soup that had been prepared the previous day. Mud still covered much of their faces and their clothes, while intact, were tattered and torn. They sat with their legs crossed in the dust while the hot Tassian suns beat down on their exhausted heads.

Casika sat too, with her back against a wooden post, and propped her knees up to support a clipboard. After several hundred interviews, she was used to the silence and simply reflected it back on her subjects until they were ready to speak. Often, it wasn't a resistance to labor that kept them from talking, but a fear of the enemy they had just escaped from.

"You don't know what they're capable of," one of them finally replied. "My son..." she trailed off, quickly interrupted by the other.

"They took our sons, our husbands. They dragged them from our houses. We watched them get executed." Both women began to sob, the first spurned on by the second.

Casika waited in silence as tears rolled from their faces and onto the dusty ground below.

"They shot them in the streets. All of them," the first woman cut in again. Sadness turned to anger as she spoke. "They're monsters. Monsters without care or compassion. What do they want? What could they want?"

"They want what you have," Casika finally responded. "They want your stuff, your home, your furniture. All of it. They want it all for themselves. But they don't just want your stuff. They want you too." Casika always made it a point to stare newcomers in the eyes when she said the last part. "They want you dead and buried. They hate you. We have to stop them."

The exhausted women returned their eyes to their soup and each stirred the contents with a spoon, allowing steam to drift up into their faces and bask their nostrils with the scent of their first meal in days. "We can fight," one of them said eventually. "We can both fight."

After collecting personal information, gathering details on family and known health concerns, Casika sent the women to Cale, Remmel's son and the chief in charge of training the rebel forces for a counterattack. In the first days following her arrival, refugees poured in and the camp had to aggressively expand its borders to make room for the people. Huts were erected overnight and, while not sufficient for long term, the huts kept weary outcasts from the rain, wind, and beating sun.

Now, however, it seemed a dragnet had been draped across the city. Refugees had almost entirely stopped coming. These women were the first to arrive in more than twelve hours, and Casika suspected that they had been lucky. Reports were coming in that enemy patrols had gotten closer and soon, maybe even tonight, Casika feared the enemy would find their camp.

Casika was afraid, but not for her own safety. Somewhere in the shadows, her protector, Arden, lurked. Refusing to reveal himself, the Mateen warrior remained hidden from sight, but she knew he did in fact remain, and with him hope remained also.

Strolling through the camp, Casika saw terrible things. Wounded exiles writhed in pain on their makeshift cots mere inches above the dusty ground. Without medicine or sterile bandages, many of the injuries became infected, causing their hosts to become feverish. Often times, as she passed, they would call to her, but they used names of loved ones lost as they sank deeper into delirium. Casika could not help them, so she continued on.

Others, while exhibiting no physical wounds, were too scarred emotionally to fight. Sometimes, they would jump back at the crackle of a log in the fire. Still others searched aimlessly in mud, desperately looking for the body parts of loved ones killed in the initial invasion. Despite her own experiences, Casika could never imagine the pain these people felt.

"Have you seen my son's eyes?" a frantic man pleaded to Casika as she walked by.

"I'm sorry," she responded, "I haven't."

"He needs them to see," the man continued to mutter, weeping as he pushed away dirt with his hands. "He needs them to see…"

These were the terrors of war. But there was good in the camp as well. Sometimes, as she walked, Casika spotted children playing makeshift games with one another. They would swordfight with twigs they found, or roll rocks back and forth, trying to break up one another's dirt piles. While rare, the carefree play of a child brought the greatest hope she could find that things would get better, that life would go on, and that soon the war would end.

"A society that values its children is bound for victory," a deep voice whispered from behind. It was Arden's.

Casika didn't bother turning because she knew that she wouldn't be able to see him. The Mateen warrior valued his secrecy and trusted no one. If there were enemy spies or scouts, it would be too dangerous for them to realize a Mateen soldier was with the rebels. While she wished that she could interact with him more, she appreciated how seriously he took his charge. "I'm glad you are still here," she said. "It makes me feel safer to know you are here."

"Plans for an attack have been drawn up," Arden responded, paying no attention to her compliment. She felt a hand slip something into her pocket, but she didn't reach for it. "Show the hologram to Remmel and Cale. It will detail how they can anticipate our air support for the operation. There's an in-depth timeline. Any deviations to the sequence of events will come from me directly to Remmel from this point on. Gemini has already begun preparations for the battle above."

Gemini's name sent shivers down Casika's neck. She had thought about him almost constantly since they had parted ways, but his name was never spoken. Until now, any memory of him was as fleeting as an apparition, appearing one moment and quickly dissipating the next.

Arden's presence meant more to her than he could ever know. It was an acknowledgement that the mysterious race she owed her life to still actually existed. It was the realization that she was neither dreaming, nor crazy in the days following her crash. Above all, it reinforced her hope of returning to a people that offered her an unconditional belonging and to a man who deserved her unconditional respect. "When do we start the battle down here?"

"In thirty-six hours, you and I will be sitting in the chairs of your capitol building," he whispered, but from farther away this time.

She didn't hear him leave, but she felt a breeze once again pushing against her back and knew Arden had departed. Plunging her hand into her pocket, she felt the small metallic object he had given her. She would bring it to Remmel at once.

CHAPTER TWENTY

Like a submarine cresting the surface of water, a faint, circular blue light folded upward from the fabric of the galaxy. Exiting the wormhole, three Lovac-class reconnaissance ships rose onto the spatial plane, and the crew of each ship sighed in relief. They had survived the journey beyond the knowable fabric of space time and were once again existing in the present. Like fishermen caught in a storm, ships often disappeared if something went wrong during wormhole travel. Unlike the sea on the Mateen home world, however, there was no bottom beyond space time, and no grave for the deceased to rest their souls within. Many crew members believed that lost ships simply drifted endlessly, forever stuck beyond the effects of time on the body. It was a fate worse than hell; these brave warriors were eternally doomed to sail about in the blackness beyond, never to be seen again.

The Mateen commandos of the three reconnaissance ships did survive, however, and now with control once again in their own hands, they would yet again have to rely on their training and skill to fight a living opponent rather than face an unknowable one. As the ships rose into the galaxy, a rogue planet drifting aimlessly appeared within their sights.

Mateen scouts were the best in the galaxy because they could fully communicate without once transmitting a radio signal. With all engines off, the reconnaissance vessels drifted toward the free-floating rogue planet and the two Jark artillery pieces concealed within.

Three, this is One. Sabik thought to his wingman. Sabik was an experienced pilot and an even better tactician. When he had been given the mission to destroy Jark interstellar artillery and tow one back for research, he leaped at the idea and spent every moment until launch planning the operation down to the last detail.

They had now entered phase two, direct observation. The Jarks had wisely camouflaged their artillery behind a free-floating planet three light years from the Tassian home world. The use of a rogue planet ensured that no gravitational pull from a system or the magnetic fields surrounding an active planet or star would interfere with their ability to accurately launch rounds toward a target. Ships, however, created heat signatures. Against the backdrop of this dead world, not only did the artillery's engines light up their sensitive instruments, but the two destroyers defending the Jark prize were illuminated as well.

Go One, responded his wingman. Mateen scouting parties operated in threes. And while their ships were small and maneuverable, they packed serious firepower for deep space missions in enemy-held territory.

I'm picking up two destroyers bracketing the artillery pieces inside the planet's orbit. Have you identified anything on the far side? Sabik asked. It was essential that all the potential threats be identified. The battle itself would be quick. Disable the escort destroyers, eliminate one of the artillery pieces, and capture the remaining piece. Once the destroyers had been eliminated, a tug vessel would make the jump to tow the Jark ship back to the Mateen home world.

I don't have anything else either. I see those ships though, and they've organized themselves as we suspected, responded Red Three, his wingman and senior scout. Call signs for the Mateens were simple ways to have formal discussions very briefly. The "Three" within a scouting party was the most experienced scout, but who often did not have the tactical expertise to plan a mission. The "One" was the leader and planner of the mission, but he often required greater scouting skill than his own experience allowed, hence partnering a "One" element with a "Three." The "Two" within a scouting formation was a junior pilot in the formation and like an apprentice to two masters, had a responsibility to learn the trade before becoming either a "One" or a "Three" himself.

OK, let's get into our modified arrow formation and get pulled into the planet's gravity. Red Two, keep those thrusters off until I give you the signal. Sabik's assault was textbook. The modified arrow accounted for three-dimensional space. The lead ship, Red Three in this case, would center itself on the lead enemy destroyer as they orbited the planet with an approach against the inside of the enemy. This would enable them to hug the planet and use its gravitational pull to attack from within rather than approach directly. The other two ships would bracket Red Three, one above to help disable the destroyers, and one near the planet's surface to target the artillery.

Once Sabik gave the word, Red Two would initiate a jamming device to silence Jark communication while Red Three and Red One ruptured the destroyer's command center with kinetic energy rounds firing at nearly five thousand meters per second. With advanced targeting and a payload of over one thousand kinetic energy rounds, Sabik and his crew could simultaneously target six weak points in the hull of the destroyer and move quickly to the artillery pieces.

Only after the destroyers had been disabled would the scouts fire their thrusters to engage the artillery. It would be Sabik himself, along with a dozen commandos, conducting the spacewalk to the second piece of artillery. Once onboard, they would disable the crew and guide the tug in for towing.

As planned, the three ships drifted silently into the planet's gravity and began to circumvent the rogue world as gravity itself pulled the daring Mateens closer and closer to the surface and their objective.

Watch your descent, Three.

I've got it, I'm good.

Three minutes until the destroyers will be visible. Two, put your finger near the jammer.

The ships floated silently, pulled inward against the massively dark rock that drifted aimlessly through space. As they circumvented the planet, a small glimmer of metal could be seen peeking out from the horizon.

There's the first destroyer. Wait for the second to come into view. Not too fast now.

I've got them both, thought an excited Three.

Me too. Hit it, Two!

With the push of a button, a tsunami of highly charged particles erupted outward from ship Two's engine compartment, rattling the three scout vessels and thrusting them forward toward the destroyers. Within a fraction of a second, the destroyers were hit by the same shockwave, and like wind pushing against sails, they tilted and rocked, forced by the wave of highly charged energy to expose their underbellies and the command centers that rested within.

Through his viewer, Sabik could see his wingman had already released his missiles, and a red light on his display indicated that it was his turn to fire on the farthest destroyer. For a split second, Sabik hovered his thumb over the red firing control, giving himself just enough time to consider the life that was soon to be lost, and then fired.

Suddenly a barrage of solid neutronium missiles raced from their tubes, and within seconds, the center of the ship was being torn in two by a force with greater gravitational density then the planet below. Fire erupted from the hull of the destroyer, and shards of metal and dust bounced off of his cockpit as the wave of expanding energy propelled him past the burning vessels and beyond the orbit of the planet.

Thrust! He screamed into the minds of his wingmen, jerking his own joystick to fight the power of the explosion. Fire and light shot from his ship's engines, pivoting him back toward the planet below. *One, destroy the first piece! Two, take out the second's defensive cannons!*

As soon as he thought his words, the first Jark artillery station withered and split under the immense fire power. Explosions rippled through the elongated hull of the vessel's storage compartments, indicating the rounds inside had been ignited beyond a toasty four thousand degrees. Defensive cannons from the second station fired upward. Their attack lasted four minutes and countermeasures were finally being employed by the doomed crew below.

Take those guns out, Two! Sabik thought aggressively, darting his small ship in and out of enemy fire exploding around him. From Sabik's right, he could see Red Two returning fire, systematically targeting the vessels defenses. Aware of a new threat, the explosions ceased around him and guns on the artillery vessel shifted to engage Red Two, but it was too late. A deadly barrage from both wingmen obliterated the defensive capabilities and left the now-lone vessel utterly helpless to prevent the Mateens from achieving their objective.

Boarding in five minutes, meet me at the hatch, Sabik told his commandos, hands shaking from the surge of adrenaline. The master pilot unstrapped himself from his seat and raced down the darkened corridors of his ship to join the rest of his commandos. Meeting them near the docking hatch, he smiled, zipped his black and gray jumpsuit to his chin and grabbed an advanced combat helmet from the rack.

In just a few minutes, Sabik had transitioned into his boarding suit, which consisted of a loosely fitting yet entirely airtight jumpsuit, an oxygen pack, a helmet and gloves that attached to and sealed his suit from the deadly vacuum of space, and most importantly, his weapon. The firearm he carried was a fully automatic rifle capable of firing hundreds of kinetic energy projectiles a minute, projectiles that were nearly as hard as the armor protecting his ship. The others in his party were also equipped with a variety of grenades, ammunition, and personnel-detention items to ensure that the enemy was entirely without any option but to surrender.

The crew of the doomed artillery cannon, however, never got that chance. As the ships docked and Sabik and his commandos blew a hole through the enemy hatch and stormed the vessel they found only corpses, suffocated by breaches in their hull from the previous battle. Sabik tried not to think about the final terrifying death they faced, but it did no good. Each Jark crewmember they came across had the same wide-eyed gaze, with hands clawing at his throat as he struggled to capture one last breath of oxygen.

Ship is secured, Sabik relayed to Gemini. *We're ready for the tug.*

***

"You what?" asked Cale, taken back by Casika's request.

"I want to learn how to fight so I can come with you on the assault."

Cale stared at her for a moment, startled by the request of the petite woman standing in front of him. It wasn't that she was a woman—they had recruited hundreds of female fighters—it was that she had returned to fight. She had the opportunity to disappear with the Mateens, but now she volunteered to take up arms and maybe even die.

"Why not?" he finally said, turning to take her to the firing line.

"We can use everyone we can get."

Casika smiled and followed Cale. His ruddy face and messy hair was a welcome look compared to the refugee side of the camp, and his upbeat personality was an even greater relief. Casika was exhausted from interacting with the refugees and was excited to learn something new. *Who knows, maybe I'll even be the one to win the war,* she thought with naive determination and an optimism stemming from finally feeling like she belonged with her own people.

Cale led Casika to an opening in the ground with a set of weathered stairs used to descend into the caves. "After the artillery barrage, a lot of these caves and tunnels collapsed on themselves," Cale told her as they walked down the steps. Each wooden rung creaked and groaned under their weight, and if not for the bacteria-fueled lanterns that lined the rocky walls, Casika would have surely lost her step and fallen to the dusty floor below. "When we set up camp, we began excavating the caves to see if we could gain access to some of the farms. As you probably know, we were successful, but that's not all. We needed a place to train, and where better than to fire our weapons underground to avoid detection?"

At the bottom, they circled past a series of row crops toward the back of the cavern. Sounds of gunfire echoed off the walls as they neared a small twenty-five meter long lane. Only two other shooters were practicing against metal targets on the far wall. Casika was relieved that there weren't going to be too many onlookers to see her fire a gun for the first time.

Cale picked up a long gray rifle and held it out. "Before you take this rifle, you have to understand that nobody wins the war all by him or herself," he told her. "We all fight together up there, and it gets confusing. If you point this in the wrong direction, you might kill your own people." Casika nodded, and Cale handed her the weapon. It was thick and heavy, but she liked the way it felt. It felt real. It was solid. It gave her the feeling of control and safety.

"This is a ZT-12 automatic rifle," he began. "I could point out all its features, but I think exploratory learning might be best since it's just us. Let's get behind it and send some rounds down range. After you get to shoot it a bit, I think what I'll have to tell you about the rifle itself will make more sense."

Casika nodded and felt her palms start to sweat. She was nervous but followed Cale's lead and lay down in the dust beside him, cupping the fore grip in her hand just as he showed her and pulling it snuggly against her shoulder. "Two things will change everything about where your rounds land," he told her. "You always need to squeeze the trigger slow, without jerking it, and always bring the sights to your face, not your face to your sights." He paused, and she grinned. "You ready?"

"I guess so," she said, doing her best to hide her insecurities.

Casika slowly squeezed the trigger, and the weapon rocked backward into her shoulder as the firing pin engaged the primer, launching a round out of the barrel. The muzzle flashed and dirt from the armor-piercing projectile kicked up dust from the target beyond. "Ouch," she muttered.

Cale laughed. "You did good! You're a natural," he joked. "Let's see if we can get you on the target now."

"Get me on target?" she hollered, hardly able to keep her own laughter down. "I thought you said I was good!"

Cale did his best to ignore her. "Do you…do…" But he couldn't stop laughing either, tears rolling down his cheeks. Finally, he was ready to start his teaching again. "Ah," he sighed with satisfaction. "I needed that." Casika punched his shoulder and frowned, but she wasn't actually angry. She had needed a good laugh and suspected he had too.

Back in business mode, Cale tried restarting his sentence for the third time. "Do you see that pale triangle glow through your scope?"

She nodded. She'd seen it but wasn't sure what it meant.

"That little triangle toward the bottom of your sights shows you where your round impacted. The gun is advanced enough to make the adjustments based on where you were looking." He paused to try and find the words to explain it. "Basically, it's watching your eye and the impact at the same time. Try again."

Casika looked through the sight again and tried to line the small cross at the center back on the target. She squeezed the trigger, this time refusing to be caught off guard from the rocking of the weapon, and watched the target disintegrate.

"Wow!" he shouted. "That's great!"

"I guess the gun makes the shooter?" she laughed, feeling more confident.

"Let's try a few more. Then we'll move to kneeling and standing firing positions," Cale said, still lying next to her in the dust below their compound.

Casika reloaded her weapon with Cale's help and continued firing throughout the afternoon. After a few hours, Cale had finally had enough. "I can't believe we've been down here so long," he exclaimed, adding, "I had better get back before my guys start wondering where I am. Besides, we've got an attack to plan."

Casika rose from her knee and held the rifle out to Cale. "Keep it," he said, gesturing with his hand. By tomorrow we're going to start walking toward the capitol anyways. It's best for you to get used to carrying it and become as familiar as possible with it.

"Do you think we can win?" Casika asked, suddenly feeling the weight of what she had just volunteered to do.

"What were you before all this?" Cale asked, dodging the question.

"I'm afraid to tell you…"

"Don't be. None of it matters anymore. To be honest, Casika, this invasion should have taught everyone a lesson about how we interact with one another. About how we rely on one another."

"I was a runaway," Casika blurted to Cale's visible surprise. The admission was freeing, and she suddenly felt as light as a feather. She was not just light, she was without yoke or burden and instantly fearless among her own people. "I didn't want to get married at the time, so I took off. I waited tables and lived off of scraps. My father left my mother when I was young, but only after there were seven of us. My mother had trouble feeding us, and was arranging marriage for all us girls. For pay, of course," she added bitterly.

"That's braver than what I would have done," he responded. "Our army is stronger now because of people like you." He paused, and a slight grin fell across his face. "I suppose we're all vagrants, aren't we?"

Casika smiled and slung the weapon over her shoulder. "You didn't answer my question," she teased.

Cale laughed and elbowed her as they walked together up the stairs. "If I didn't think we could win, I certainly wouldn't be bringing you along!"

"So your father is giving you the role of taking over the government sector during tomorrow's assault?" she pried, trying to glean more information about their planning.

"Yes, but there's a bigger battle going on beyond the government building." As they rose out of the ground, Casika suddenly realized that she hadn't heard the birds or insects all afternoon. The contrast between above and below was incredible, and she staggered a bit as she ascended to the surface.

Cale stopped at the top of the steps and turned to look over the city against the darkening sky. "My dad has sent some of our more advanced scouts and trainers to notify the people of a coordinated attack against the invaders. He wants Tassi to erupt like bees swarming from a hive against its attackers."

"I'm not sure I'll be able to sleep tonight," Casika said with a timid smile. "With all that's going to happen, I mean," she quickly added.

Cale laughed again. "Then your training is complete!" he said, walking away toward his father's tent. "No soldier can sleep before a battle."

Casika waited awhile longer, watching her city beyond. She was excited to stand with Cale as he freed Tassi tomorrow.

CHAPTER TWENTY-ONE

Gemini jumped from his command chair with a cheer. The men on his bridge cheered with him. "Well done, team!" he shouted exuberantly.

The mission had gone exactly as planned, and Sabik had once again proved why he was the top scout in the fleet. "Your hard work and planning led to this overwhelming success," he insisted, trying to motivate his staff. "But it isn't over yet. Phase one is complete with the seizure of those artillery stations, but we're a long way from victory." Gemini paused to let his message soak in. "Castor, alert the tugs on the far end of the system to initiate phase two. Let the feint attack begin."

Gemini walked off the bridge and into his office. In a few hours, Brokk's intelligence officers and fleet commanders would detect the seismic anomaly that had knocked out the artillery and Brokk would suspect something was wrong. It was absolutely essential that Gemini retain the upper hand against the Jarks and maintain his momentum.

Ever since he was a young officer in the fleet, he clung to four principals of offensive maneuver to dictate his entire strategy. He recited them now in his head as he rehearsed the plan to ensure he hadn't forgotten anything.

Surprise. He had achieved surprise with the assault on the artillery and would achieve it again with his feint attack against their defenses.

Concentration. He would concentrate his firepower against their main defense, using the asteroid tug as a diversion but not a diversion of firepower. This allowed all of his forces to focus on fighting and avoided his requirement to divide them on the flanks.

Audacity. When executed boldly, Brokk would never suspect that the Mateens would attack so early and so violently. They certainly wouldn't expect a dead sprint to the center planet from the asteroid belt. War just wasn't fought that way—at least, it shouldn't be.

Tempo. He would keep up the pace to ensure they reacted to him, not the other way around.

Satisfied, Gemini returned to the bridge. Castor greeted him. "Tugs have initiated movement," he said, pulling up the holographic image of the solar system onto the viewing screen. "You can see the heat signatures here. Our own systems were surprised and alerted us to a potential vessel exiting the asteroid belt. If it fooled us, it's bound to fool them."

Gemini smiled. On the screen, two yellow outlines of unknown ships moved out of the asteroid belt and inward toward their enemy. To replicate life on the ships, the robotic tugs were given several hundred heated dummies. The engineering team also drilled four ion propulsion generators into the asteroid's surface to give computers the illusion of thrust. With a five-hundred-meter cable attaching the rock to the tug, the footprint of the vessels on their radar was about two thousand meters long and gave the impression of a battleship.

Gemini was happy, but he wasn't out of the woods yet. Synchronizing this battle was easy because he controlled the entire fleet. It was Gemini who dictated pace and positioning. The ground fight was an entirely different story, and Gemini desperately hoped that they would be able to launch the large-scale rebellion he needed to send the Jark soldiers running.

***

"This is excellent news, Commander Brokk."

In the darkened office space, a council of nine holographic Jark officials sat in a U-shaped pattern around Brokk's desk. The Jark ruler was displayed directly across from him at the end of the table. He was a large, pureblood Jark with red skin and dark black hair covering most of his body. His lips curled as he sat listening to the other members of his council bombard Brokk with questions about the living conditions, timeline for settlement, and known threats. Finally, the ruler cut in with a grunt to let the council know that it was his turn to speak.

"What about the refugee?" he snarled. "What about the Mateens?"

Brokk knew the topic was going to come up, but he had still hoped it wouldn't. "They'll respect the decision of the Galactic Council," Brokk said nonchalantly.

The ruler growled and slammed his fist into his black desk, which had been forged out of the sulfuric iron ore that constantly oozed to Jark's surface. Ripples echoed through the hologram in Brokk's own office at the force of the ruler's outburst. "They're at the council right now trying to build a coalition for war!" he shouted. "How could you let her escape?"

Brokk said nothing. Deep inside, he hated the ruler. He was a filthy man whose greed for control clouded his judgment. Brokk believed that he had no right to rule the Jarkian people. He had no right to rule over Brokk. But Brokk had needed an army, and the ruler had given him one.

"Well?" he growled in a voice that started low in his abdomen and erupted from his throat with such fervor it startled the nearby councilmen.

"Would you like for me to go destroy them as well?" Brokk finally said. "Send me more ships and I'll wage this war too. Otherwise, I'm certain someone in your cabinet can handle the Mateens politically while we tighten our grip here on Tassi."

"Don't patronize me, Brokk," the ruler retorted. "I'll be with you soon and any difficulty this causes for me will be met with severe punishment against you and your commanders."

Brokk suspected that the ruler was jealous and wanted to ensure that no one would be eager to forsake him to follow Brokk. "Tassi will be..."

But Brokk was unable to smooth things over. Just as he was prepared to complete his sentence by saying that *Tassi would be just as the ruler desired it,* Terre flew through the door.

"Commander!" Terre exclaimed, panting from climbing the steps to his office. "We've lost contact with our artillery and Lago is reporting two unknown battleships closing in on his position from the asteroid belt."

"We'll have to finish this discussion another time," Brokk said to a wide-eyed cabinet. Brokk shut the screen off as the ruler was shouting something about not disconnecting them. Brokk didn't care. The battle was what he lived for. "Take me to my ship and get Lago on the radio," he said to Terre, flying out of his seat and up the steps to the roof toward his shuttle launchpad.

CHAPTER TWENTY-TWO

Lago could hardly contain his excitement as he rushed toward the bridge of his battleship to command his forces against an oncoming enemy assault. The strategy of employing weapons in the offense was enjoyable, but the defense was far better. It was in the defense that he got to test all of his preparations against a willing enemy commander.

For days, Lago had moved and adjusted sensors to make sure that each and every spot had been accounted for. When that was complete, he had tirelessly examined dead spots in space that didn't have weapon systems that could engage it, and he would find a weapon system that could. Once that was complete, his men would practice over and over again until Lago was absolutely certain that they understood their role in the fight.

Not even this stopped Lago's incessant preparation, however. At night, when he couldn't sleep but also couldn't stand the thought of searching for his soul, Lago would go back through his maps and plans for defending the planet against a counterattack and compared them against the known tactics of his enemies. Now, coming out of the asteroid belt, two battleships seemed to be willing to test his preparations.

"Are they Tassian?" he asked, arriving at his command center.

"We aren't sure," his intelligence officer responded. "The two ships are certainly large enough to be more of the Tassian fleet that we had destroyed previously, but they would have been hiding in the belt for a long time. It doesn't look like they originated from another planet within the system."

"What's their speed?" Lago asked. It was surprising that someone would be bold enough to launch a frontal assault from so far away against his formation. Lago was suspicious, but as he studied the computer readings, he agreed. These were two battleships, and they were headed straight for his armada.

"They're moving slow but picking up speed. I'm measuring fifteen thousand kilometers per second, but our systems are projecting that they'll likely increase to twenty by the time they are within range."

"That's slow, isn't it?" Lago asked, yet again perplexed at the tactic. "How fast should a Tassian battleship be able to go?" he wondered out loud. His crew, however, didn't respond. They had their computer-generated readings, and he agreed—these did appear to be battleships.

Lago sat in his chair and pondered the map. Nothing was simple, not on the ground and certainly not here in space. In the defensive line, he had much better odds, but two battleships still posed a formidable threat. Lago looked at his forces arrayed against his foe. He had three battleships, six destroyers, and nearly twenty reconnaissance ships. If

Brokk had received his message, he might get Brokk's battleship as well, leaving him with four, six, and twenty against their two. They didn't stand a chance. They couldn't.

"How long until they are within range?" Lago asked.

"Ten minutes, sir."

"Good. Maneuver destroyers One-Two and One-Three from the far side of Tassi so they can be in a better position to engage. I want them orbiting the bright side of the moon to use as cover. Provide battleship One on the far side of Tassi to offer them support."

The Jark naming convention gave destroyers all double-digit numbers to signify what battle group they belonged to. One-Two and One-Three, for instance, belonged to battleship One. Lago had Battleships One, Two, and Three, each with two destroyers assigned to them.

"Do you think that'll be enough, Lago?" his first officer challenged. "If these are Tassian battleships on a suicide run, destroyers might not have the firepower to take them out."

Lago remained silent as he pondered the advice. Something was wrong, he knew it, but he couldn't pluck it out of the void beyond. Sparing any additional ships would take them out of formation from the overall defense and cause him difficulty responding to any additional threat. Still, though, his first officer had a point. If these guys were desperate, they would set their computers to autopilot so that they could fight until every weapon system has been depleted, with or without oxygen for the crew.

"Everybody is looking toward the threat," he said quietly.

"What's that?" his first officer responded.

"It's a trap. It has to be! Scan the asteroid belt for additional ships. Anything that looks strange. Push our scouts out from the planet. Something's off. If I'm wrong, fine, let's move our ship into a position where we can fire from this distance. I don't want to leave our side of Tassi, but if we need to provide the extra firepower, I would rather it be us than anyone else."

His crew acknowledged this order, and Lago suddenly found himself doubting everything he had established in the defense.

***

"There!" Gemini shouted as he watched the map relaying information about the Jark fleet. "That's four out of nine thrusting toward the threat!" Gemini was excited. This was what he lived for. He looked at his watch. In nineteen minutes the ground assault would begin and he had to have both the fleet and Brokk distracted enough up here to make victory possible. There could be absolutely no interference from the Jark fleet against Remmel's ground troops.

While nineteen minutes might seem like a short amount of time, Gemini knew that in the vacuum of space, nineteen minutes was an eternity. Gemini eyed Castor and received a nod. *We're all set. The Armada is awaiting your command.*

"Enemy ships approaching our position," shouted his radar operator. "Scouts."

Gemini turned to find his seat and took it. "Strap in boys," he told his staff. "There's no need to keep it quiet. We'll engage the scouts. I want battle group One's fighters to begin knocking out sensors. Destroyers and battleships, defend those fighters from additional reconnaissance vessels conducting patrols. Battle group Two and our group will head right for the heart of Tassi. Two, take out those ships targeting our tugs orbiting along the western hemisphere of the main planet. I count at least three with a possible fourth. After we destroy the scouts, my ship will spearhead the assault against the two battleships in the center and their respective fighters."

Gemini paused to take one final look around his crew. The staff on his bridge all looked at him expectedly. Inside his mind, there were thousands of others from the armada waiting for his guidance. *Thrusters to maximum,* he thought to his collective.

In space, the ability to direct the thrust of a vessel was the singular most important aspect of battlefield maneuverability. It was irrelevant how small or large a ship was or whether it looked like a sphere or a triangle. Thrust was the difference; the ability of powerful engines to stop your vessel in its tracks and change course just as quickly was the sole discriminator in this deadly game of chess.

It only took fifteen seconds for the void of space to pull every last ounce of oxygen from a man's veins. This was a sprint, and Gemini and his crew of heroes had seven billion kilometers to sprint before their enemy found a way to outthrust them.

Out of the asteroid belt, twenty gray Mateen warships and hundreds of planetary fighters erupted from their starting positions like horses on a racetrack. Even in a gravity-free environment, Gemini's body sunk into the chair as his vessel exerted more force on his bones and muscles than he could ever remember before. Traveling at over forty thousand kilometers per second, the enemy ships would be in range in four minutes.

Already, Gemini could see explosions on his screen from the destruction of the farthest beacons and sensors that the Jark forces had deployed to dampen Mateen warp capability. It was irrelevant; he had punched through instead.

Solar artillery now online, reported his fire support officer.

Don't wait for my approval, Gemini responded.

Suddenly, dust lines from proximity rounds launched from his cannons hiding in the asteroid belt and onward to their targets beyond. It had begun.

***

"The battleships will be in range in fifteen seconds," announced Lago's targeting officer. Since the two vessels departed the asteroid belt, they hadn't made a single course adjustment. They were two ships on a suicide mission. Lago was happy to oblige.

"Bring us about," he responded. "I want to watch this on the viewing screen.

As the screen clicked on, the crew waited with anticipation. On his map he could see the two icons inching forward toward the moon and the waiting ambush. They were his two destroyers, lions crouching in a field as they stalked their prey.

Suddenly, he could see it. The small gray nose of a warship began to peek out from behind the moon. "Zoom in," he ordered, magnifying his optical screen to see the battle. As soon as it magnified, Lago's heart almost stopped. It wasn't a battleship. It was a tug, and in its grasp was an asteroid.

"Spin us around!" he ordered. Panic filled his thoughts as his crew rushed to correct their mistake. "Ambush!" shouted Lago to his armada. "It's an ambush. Get back to your primary defensive positions!"

But it was too late. As his ship turned, the seismic bursts of proximity munitions erupted around him, jostling the massive battleship and frustrating his efforts to maneuver or gain thrust against the attacking enemy to his rear.

"Primary thrusters just went out!" shouted his pilot.

"Fire the landing dampeners. We have to turn about!" Lago ordered as he struggled to gain his balance and get back to his command chair. "Get Commander Brokk on the PTS!"

CHAPTER TWENTY-THREE

Remmel and Cale stood side by side, overlooking the city from their wetland hideout. They hadn't spoken since they had arrived nearly ten minutes earlier, instead favoring silent companionship to verbal communication.

"The city is still beautiful," Remmel said at last.

The moment was eerie. Like a blackened sky before a violent storm, Cale knew there was a chance that he would never see his father again. "It is," he finally said. "It's worth fighting for. Worth dying for."

Remmel finally turned and looked at his son, putting a hand on his shoulder. "I remember when I went to combat for the first time," he said somberly. "My dad met me at the shuttle that was going to transport us out to the front. He didn't say anything, just stuck his hand out and I shook it." Remmel paused, reflecting on the past. "I'll never forget that. There was so much in that handshake that probably should have been said—that could have been said."

Cale, who had kept his eyes fixed on the horizon, finally broke his gaze and looked at his father. "Were you scared?" he asked.

"Terrified," he responded. "But not because I was worried about dying. That never even crossed my mind. I wasn't a coward. I was worried that I would make the wrong decision. I was worried that I wouldn't be able to lead my men."

Cale laughed a bit to cover his nervousness. "That's how I feel."

"I'm proud of you, Cale. This battle is yours for the taking." Remmel pointed toward the sky. "For two hours now there has been a different fight raging up there. The people fighting aren't doing it for themselves. They're doing it for you, for our people. They believe in you, in us. I do too."

Cale looked toward the ground. His father was right, and the implications were far greater than just Cale and his company of infantry. Even as they spoke, millions of Tassians were arming themselves in their homes. Millions of Tassians were ready to win back their world; they were relying on Cale, and Cale was relying on the Mateens. "I just don't want to lose anyone," he said at last.

"I know. But remember: The worst thing you can do is fail to make a decision," responded Remmel. "Remember that always. Your company of two hundred can accomplish anything, even if they are running head on into fire. As long as your company is doing it quickly and with the same breath, nothing can stop them. As soon as indecision creeps in, your men will get confused, they will fight slowly, you'll get outmaneuvered, and you'll lose a lot of them." Remmel held his gaze a moment longer. "You are smart and capable. This battle is yours."

Cale nodded and gave his father a slight smile. "Thanks. We're going to take back the city now." He put his hand out to shake his father's but was instead wrapped up in a hug. They held it for a long time, and Cale refused to be the one to let go. Finally, he felt his father loosen his grip.

"I'll be right here when you get back," Remmel said, pushing him away and down the hill.

Cale walked slowly at first but then let the gravity pull him down faster and faster until he was running at a near sprint. Below, he could see the members of his formation checking their weapons and smearing mud on their faces to conceal themselves in the brush during the movement to their objective. In the back was Casika, donning the camouflage of the Mateen space fleet that she had first arrived with. He was glad that she was there.

As Cale approached his formation, they all turned to watch him. It was time. This victory was theirs, and Cale was ready to lead them.

CHAPTER TWENTY-FOUR

Commander Brokk, soon to be chancellor of the Tassian system, waited impatiently on the roof of his captured government building with Terre for a shuttle that should have arrived by now. "What's taking them so long?" he asked impatiently.

Terre shrugged. "I'm sure Lago can handle it, Commander." He paused. "But you're right. I'll make sure your crew understands its priorities. Your ability to get back to your ship under any circumstance is paramount."

Brokk sighed. The dual suns beat down violently against his face, and his eyes strained in the light. It was painful and he was sick of squinting. "Just get them on the radio and find out what the holdup…" Brokk stopped. Something caught his attention. A flash of light. A rumble. The noise of an explosion.

Brokk raced to the edge of the building toward the sound, toward the swamp. Suddenly, gunfire erupted from the tree line against his checkpoints below.

An attack. A coordinated attack, he thought as gunfire echoed off the buildings and flashed in the streets.

"Get our air support over here!" Brokk shouted, running for the stairs to get to his command center so that he could direct the fight.

Just as he reached them, an explosion ripped off a corner of his building and shook the crystal structure so violently that Brokk struggled to keep his balance. Looking up, he could see enemy fighters fill the sky. They were gray and angular with the triangular wing structure that meant only one thing: They were Mateen.

Brokk regained his balance and raced the forty stories down toward the control center of the government building. Flying through the door, he was met with a flurry of reports. "Not all at once!" he screamed to silence his operations center. "Let's work from the top down. Space Ops, what's the status of the battle above?"

A gray-haired Jark pressed a button to bring up his display for the rest of the team to see. Two Jark battleships and three destroyers were all that remained on his screen. It looked as if they had arrayed themselves in a diagonal line to face the horde of Mateen warships while maintaining a three-dimensional formation within space.

"Lago's battleship is here and next to it is yours. Your shuttle is still en route, but when Lago realized what he was up against, he ordered your ship to break orbit to assist with the battle." The officer circled an area in the asteroid field with his hand. "The Mateen armada concealed themselves here and launched a full-frontal assault when Lago adjusted his perimeter to counter a feint attack." He paused again, but just before Brokk could shout at him to speed it up, he continued.

"One battleship and three destroyers have been lost. It's unclear if we've inflicted any damage on the Mateens at this point, but reports are still pouring in."

"Fine," responded Brokk. "Close air support. You're next," he said, motioning to the next man at the table. "You'd better have a good explanation for why a missile blew up the side of my building."

A second Jark rose, tearing a headset off of the top of his head so that he could speak. "Two of the three battleships were able to deploy their planetary fighters. Lago ordered one group to remain in space to help against the assault but diverted the other group once we realized the Mateen intention was to provide their own air support to the rebel counterattack."

"What are the numbers?" asked Brokk hastily.

"We're outnumbered two to one," he responded solemnly.

"We've got air defense here on the ground. Get it up and running. There's no reason why we wouldn't fill the air with missiles," Brokk ordered.

"It'll interfere with…" the man started to counter before dodging a paper book thrown by Brokk.

"Do it! Ground force commander. What have you got?"

"We're getting pummeled," said a third Jark plainly. He was a tall ogre of a man with scars from previous battles still speckling his face. He was wearing the traditional green-and-brown camouflage of an infantryman and had his armor on as well. "If we don't regain air superiority soon, my positions won't last. We'll fight to the end, but we won't last."

Brokk was ready to heed this man's advice. Unlike the other two, Brokk had known Canis from previous wars and knew that he was the real deal. "What about bringing fighters in from other parts of the city?" he asked.

"We've got the men, but they're being hit everywhere. It's a coordinated attack across the country. Somehow the people managed to rearm themselves right under our noses...and they aren't conventional munitions. These have been supplied by someone. When they aren't being attacked from the air, the people are revolting on every street on the planet. My men have their hands tied."

The Mateens are behind this. Brokk stood silently, waiting to see if Canis had more. He did. "There's a command center coordinating this. I've sent a brigade to find them."

"Where?" Brokk asked.

"We think they're in the marshlands, between the capital and the sea. It's likely a fool's errand and will doubtfully affect the rebellion that is now in full swing, but perhaps we'll get our revenge." He looked at his own hands as he gripped his weapon. "I'm going out there to command the defense of this building, but if we don't win the air, we won't win the ground."

Brokk nodded as Canis walked past and allowed himself a moment to study the map. Sensors on Jark uniforms automatically reported locations of people shooting at them and populated the locations on the map above, a three dimensional holographic orb that spanned all of Tassi. Like a beehive awakened from its rest, the red dots far outweighed his blue, and they swarmed.

He examined the space battle again. Against so many Mateen warships above, there would be no hope of victory, even if Canis's men did find a way to destroy the enemy command center Brokk was certain the Mateens wouldn't give up. After they had gained air superiority, they would turn their bombers to against his ground troops and there would be no escape.

On the ground, the enemy on the map was so pervasive, he could hardly see his own soldiers. In space, Lago's formation was broken, and only two battleships remained, his and Lagos. They were stretched too thin, and now a deadly game of cat and mouse was developing as Lago piloted his ship to the far side of the Tassian moon in the face of the Mateen horde.

"Is the Empire sending reinforcements?" his space officer asked.

"No," Brokk muttered. "We're on our own."

The Jarks on his staff stopped what they were doing at looked at him. It was over. They all knew it. But Brokk wouldn't return home. He couldn't. He would be put to death for this. They all would be. And they knew it. The ruler had failed the political game; allowed a third race to enter the war uncontested, and would let Brokk take the fall. *But how could we die for a ruler who would just as quickly sell us out to our enemies? How could we possibly sacrifice any more than we already have for a nation that will sacrifice nothing on our behalf?*

"Fight to the death," he finally ordered. "Consolidate our force on the government quarter. Hold them off until we find their command and control element and eliminate it. Where's my shuttle, Terre?"

"It just arrived," he shouted from behind.

"Good, you're flying. We've got to rescue Lago. This battle is still ours to lose. Divert all planetary fighters to the planet's surface to provide close air support. Defend the capitol, divide their forces, kill every citizen that refuses to surrender." Terre acknowledged, and the two raced out the doors to get to his shuttle, but Brokk halted. He had just remembered his priests. "Tell the priests," he said, looking back to his operations officer, "tell them to release the grootslang."

***

Explosions burst all around Remmel as he scrambled out of his olive-green command tent and dove into a ditch. The familiar whistles of incoming mortars followed by their subsequent eruptions as metallic shells impacted the sandy soil of his operations center indicated a counterattack, something he had feared but refused to acknowledge as a possibility. Reaching the ditch line as another shell detonated above, Remmel scurried on his elbows and knees along the V-shaped trench to get to the front, where he could direct the soldiers who had remained to defend the refugees from this very possibility.

"Keep your heads down!" he shouted, crawling past men gripping machine guns. "Keep them down! The attack is coming and we've got to be alive to fight them off!"

Remmel knew what would come next. Hundreds of Jark soldiers were going to come pouring at them from the tree line in front of his trench and attempt to kill everyone they could find. To make matters worse, the old commander had chosen to minimally man his outpost, favoring instead to send as many as people as he could to seize the government quarter of the city. Now, the risk of losing his operations center was materializing before his very eyes, and he began to wonder if he had miscalculated the ferocity of his attack. If the Jarks could spare the men to attack his outpost, perhaps not as many took to the streets as he had calculated.

Finally, Remmel reached the tip of the trench line that faced the city and divided his camp from the enemy. "When the barrage stops, get up and watch for the assault!" he shouted to two grimy-faced soldiers who manned the main defensive cannon; neither looked up as fresh shrapnel mixed with sand and rocks rained down on their helmets from above.

After each volley, Remmel counted to ten. If more rounds came in before then, he knew the attack was not yet upon them. This time, however, he got to ten and the dread of the reality of trench warfare nearly paralyzed him. Seconds ticked by as an eerie silence engulfed the camp. *The peace before a storm.*

"Heads up!" he bellowed, jumping to his feet with his rifle and propping it over the top of the trench. Lights flashed from the row of trees as bullets snapped past him and kicked up dirt into his eyes. "Light it up!" he shouted, eager to hear the hammering of their own automatic weapons erupt all around him.

Remmel knew that the back and forth was only an intermediary stage to the rush, and he reserved firing his own weapon for when the Jarks exposed themselves from the tree line. Despite the heavy barrage of Tassian cannons, the fearless beasts finally launched from their hiding places in a bid to take the encampment.

Aiming his weapon at the first knuckle-dragging Jark he saw, Remmel squeezed his trigger and watched the round from his semiautomatic rifle smash through the body of an eager enemy warrior. It didn't bring him any satisfaction, however, and while Remmel continued firing, a rock grew inside his stomach with each life he took.

Despite the effort of his men, there were far more Jarks than there were Tassians, and soon his enemy had courageously fought to within a few hundred meters from his line. "Pour it on them!" he shouted, running from position to position, careful to keep his head low and his body hunched to stay below the rounds that flew over his position.

"We're out!" screamed a machine gun team to his left. "Black on ammo!"

Remmel surveyed his thinly manned line. Already he had men and women reeling in the trench from bullet wounds and nearly half of his positions were out of ammo. To his front, the Jarks were preparing another push for the trench.

"Fall back!" Remmel shouted into his radio.

This was a planned withdrawal and best done now before it became a hasty one. Their defenses consisted of three V-shaped trenches, each with an equal number of machine gun positions. As they exhausted their ammunition, they would withdraw to the second trench three hundred meters behind the first and continue the fight—but after three, it was going to be a bloody battle to the end.

Jark soldiers jumped up again and rushed his line only to be beaten back by machine gun fire from the second trench, and with this small victory, hope dwindled for the infantry on both sides as a second barrage of mortars began to fall on the Tassian position. Thus was the desperate back and forth of trench warfare, and Remmel could only hope that his mighty warriors would have what it took to hold the enemy horde at bay.

CHAPTER TWENTY-FIVE

Light shimmered off of the mercury-infused wading pool and danced lazily between the darkened crystal walls and white tiled floors in the basement of the government building. Canis never came down this far and didn't ever plan to. The priests and their rituals were not for him, and he had little interest in their work. In fact, the twenty-year Jark infantry veteran considered many of their rituals barbaric and unnecessary, mere superstitions that only served to arouse fear in their own people rather than achieve victory over their enemies.

Thinking back to the infant sacrifice prior to battle, he tried to make sense of their present circumstances and of the leaders who so eagerly accepted the sign as from beyond the grave. He'd seen many sacrifices but had never understood any of them. Canis was in charge of his own destiny, not the dead.

As he rounded the short hallway that separated the stairwell from the pool, he could instantly see them. Six priests, dressed in long golden robes, stood motionless around the pool. They uttered not a word as he came in and seemed not to notice him, even as he approached the chief priest's position at the head of the rectangular room. Canis, unsure of how to get their attention, watched for a moment before finally clearing his throat to announce his presence.

None looked up. All six remained stoic and motionless, with golden hoods covering their eyes making it impossible to judge their thoughts or intentions. After another moment, one spoke, the only one whose tongue remained. "Child!" he hissed in a frail whisper. His voice was horse and shaky. "You have a message for us?"

"The grootslang," returned Canis. "You are to release it. I've been ordered to ensure that you do." Canis lowered his head to search for the eyes and mouth of the speaker who hid beneath his cowl, but he could find none. The six remained still, as if statues sculpted as part of the room, basking in the same silver light as the walls and floor.

"The grootslang," the priest responded. "Is he certain?" A tinge of fear dripped from his vaporous words and hung in the air long after the priest had asked his question.

"He is. The Tassians making one final push for the planet. Brokk wants this to be left for the Tassians as a gift."

"Ahhhh," said the priest, releasing decades of stale air from his decrepit lungs. "Yet I see that you doubt us."

"It matters not," responded the career soldier, angered by the priest's accusation.

"It matters a little," he whispered back. "But you'll soon believe."

"I don't care," Canis said, louder this time. "Once you've released the beast, I will evacuate you."

"We do not leave the pool," he hissed. "And the beast will consume us all!"

Fervor erupted from the old man's face, and now Canis could see his eyes as he lifted his head toward the crystal ceiling and raised his arms. His eyes glowed a deep gold that matched the colors of their robes. In unison, the men began their chant to bring forth the serpent from another time, the serpent that would *consume* them all.

Canis turned to leave. He wanted no part of this, but something gripped him. His arms were pinned by an invisible moisture that wrapped him like a spider spinning a web and pulled him toward the chief priest. "Where?" demanded the chief priest, "are you going? You are the sacrifice!"

Mercury bubbled and boiled to the ritualistic chants that grew ever louder. The invisible chains became visible; metallic vapors that rose from the very pool itself squeezed the terrified Jark.

"Let me go!" Canis struggled, but his strength failed him. All he could do was watch in horror as a black arc rose slowly from the pool. Slowly at first, but suddenly, all at once, the blackness rose with a hungry haste. From the arc a head appeared and then fangs. The priests chanted onward, and the beast rose higher and higher into the air. Twenty feet. Thirty. Mercury dripped out of its mouth and off its fangs as they hung, suspended from massive jaws connected to a thick snakelike body. The grootslang.

The priests were shouting their chant now, but even their voices trembled as the beast rose from the murky depths of the wading pool. Then, without cue from their master, the shouting stopped. Silence gripped the room, and even Canis dared not let out even a breath. He could only watch.

Its eyes were closed at first but a thin reddish tongue slipped slowly from its mouth. It smelled its environment. It smelled Canis. Suddenly, the skin covering its eyes opened and the golden pupils of a thirty-foot tall demon spotted its first meal.

***

Fighters streaked across the bright blue sky, dropping hundreds of bombs on their targets below. Casika watched as gray Mateen bombers dodged the red colored Jark fighters in a desperate bid to control the air. Mateen fighters, smaller than the wide bodied bombers swarmed in and out of formations, swooping to attack an enemy ship and rolling hard to avoid enemy fire.

Explosions erupted all around Casika and Cale as Jark bombers countered their efforts with clusters of their own munitions; sending Cale's company scattering in the muddy marsh as explosion after explosion shook the muddied ground.

"You OK?" Cale asked, grabbing her arm and shouting into her temporarily tone deaf ears.

Mud dripped from Casika's face. She pushed herself up. Grit and dirt ground between her teeth. Heat from the nearby explosion was still hot against her skin. Fire simmered beyond the small log that had barely sheltered her from the burst.

"I think so," she responded, accepting his help and climbing to her knees; searching for and grabbing her rifle that was buried in the mud at an arm's length away.

"Don't lose that," Cale said to her, "That's your life."

Shamed. Casika felt her cheeks surge with blood. They had been walking all morning and her body was heavy under the extra weight of the rifle and ammunition. *Clumsy,* she thought again. But no time to dwell. Engines roared above. The water vibrated below.

"Another sortie," Cale shouted, "get your heads down!"

Casika threw herself back into the cold wet water, feeling it soak into her clothes and sending shivers back up her spine. Mud squished underneath her legs as she sank back into the swamp. Cale covered her body with his. Another blast rocked the marsh. More heat burned against her arm.

"Time to go," he said pulling her up once more. "We can't let their planes slow our advance."

Casika wearily watched the veteran soldiers fall back into line and continue their march towards the government sector. Mud dripped from their faces. Black rifles were brown from dirt. *How can these men possibly be ready to fight after this,* she wondered.

"How much farther until the city?" she asked Cale who stood by her side, watching his men continue their movement.

"Another hour maybe," was his response. He grinned white teeth through a grime and sweat covered face. "Depends who wins the sky."

Depends on who wins the sky. Casika mulled Cale's comment over and over again in her mind as she trudged through the mud towards higher ground and the government sector. Insects swarmed her head and threatened to bite at the exposed skin on her face and head. The marsh stunk. Dirty brown water swirled around her feet and who knew what else lay beneath the water. *Don't think about it. Keep moving.* The company pressed on. *Depends.*

During the planning, Casika had never considered Cale's statement. *Depends.* She never considered there might not be a Mateen victory; air support might dwindle, the Jarks might retake control. Their assault might be in vain. *Worse than in vain. Dead. All of them. Maybe not just dead but executed; thrown from the same building as the chancellor and his cabinet. Imprisoned, tortured, then killed. Dead.*

Don't think that way, she scorned herself. *Dead is better than it was before. Dead for a people that accepts you is better than life alone. Life with nothing. Life stealing water and food from the rich and then hating them for it. Dead is good rather than life with the Jarks.*

The column stopped and Casika, staring at her feet, bumped into the soldier to her front. "Pay attention," he hissed.

"Why are we stopping?"

The soldier didn't respond, instead after seeing a hand signal from another man, he took off at a sprint to his right and took a knee. Suddenly, Casika realized where they were. The edge of the marsh. The start of the city; the start of the real fighting.

Cale wasted no time pushing his formation out of the woods and onto the street. The men moved slowly at first, cresting the small hill on their stomachs and then running to the nearest building, a red bricked warehouse that marked the edge of the city. Casika watched the first man kick a red door open on the corner of the structure and a column of nine soldiers rush through. Silence.

"Roll and peel," a mud covered soldier whispered to Casika, startling her as she focused on the street.

"What?"

"It's your turn," he responded, gesturing toward the road. "Crawl up to the edge, make sure it's clear, and peel off into the building. We've secured it as our foothold into the city."

"Foothold?" she asked.

"Just get to that red door," he ordered.

OK," she responded stepping forward but feeling his grip still on her shoulder.

"Hey, make sure you look up before you go too."

She nodded. *Look up. No planes.* At the edge of the trees the bright blue sky had returned from a few days ago during the initial attack. She could still see the cuts and tears in her mind; black ovals forming as artillery from another world flew through. Casika stepped out. *Solid ground.* Water drained from her boots and pooled on the concrete; relief flooded through her heart and lungs to be out of the swamp and back in the city. *To be home.*

"Run," a hushed shout boomed from behind.

And she did. A full sprint from the trees to the red brick building. Hurtle the gray curb separating the street from the sidewalk. Water logged pants and boots splashed muddy swamp sludge against the street as she jumped; staining it in brown. She felt heavy but the adrenaline surged through her veins as the sound of engines above thundered off the walls. *Warplanes.*

Twenty feet, get inside before they see you. A red door swung open and Cale stepped out. "Hurry!" he shouted.

Ten feet. Not far. Don't trip. The rifle rocked against her hip and was heavy on her shoulder. Her feet ached as they smashed against the hard pavement. Engines roared overhead. The shadow of a plane appeared against the building.

Casika didn't care who's side the plane was on. Mateen or Jark, it didn't matter. *Get inside and get in quick.* Without looking up she dove into Cale's outstretched arm and flung herself through the door. *Safe. Maybe.*

Cale didn't check to see if she was okay. Always focused on the mission he climbed a set of metallic steps and once at the top, he walked to large window panes on the front of the warehouse and looked out.

"Get snipers on top of this room," he ordered his men. "I want you to clear the streets. Cover our movement." He turned to face the men that had gathered on the first floor of the warehouse. "We aren't staying here. Let's get back out. I can see the government building from here. It's covered in black. Let's liberate it."

The men grunted in unison. Casika shuddered, unsure if she had the energy to go back out on the streets.

CHAPTER TWENTY-SIX

Panting, Casika dove behind a building as bullets the size of her hand tore off a corner off brick and sent it shattering against the back of her head. In two blocks time, the streets had filled with soldiers and civilians on both sides of the battle. Jark infantry were clearing homes and setting up machine guns inside windows to slow their enemy's advance. Citizens armed with Mateen weapons shot back. In the middle, Cale and his soldiers pushed from block to block, gaining inches of ground before turning down another street.

"Let the Jarks deal with the uprising!" he shouted. "Keep pushing to the center. Karath," he ordered. "Push west. Clear the last street."

Cale was practicing a deliberate envelopment of the structure, knowing that the Jarks would fight the hardest to retain this essential piece of real estate. With Karath's unit moving west, a perimeter had been set, and all that remained to keep them from their prize was a group of thirty Jark fighters who had dug into positions around the building itself.

As security suppressed the embattled enemy at the flank, Cale maneuvered his assault force as close as possible.

"Having fun yet?" Cale shouted as her helmet smashed into his while the building shook behind them. A grenade exploded to their front and rained down dirt onto her arms and legs. *Chaos. This is complete chaos.* She couldn't speak. *Just move,* she thought. *Keep moving.*

Cale didn't wait for a response and instead turned to order his more experienced squad leader to their next fighting position.

"Get that machine gun back up!" he shouted, leaning over the body of a dead Tassian soldier. "Empty your grenades! We're almost there. You," he pointed at another, "get short range mortars on those roof tops. Make it rain!"

"How much farther?" she shouted at him, afraid to get up and look through the nearly constant exchange of rifle fire.

"Thirty meters! Wait for the support position to start firing again and we'll make our final dash!"

Thirty meters. Thirty meters for the rest of their lives. They had made it so far and the prize was within reach. Thirty meters. Casika took a deep breath and gripped her rifle, unsure if she could actually use it against another. Suddenly, the rhythmic thumping of heavy machine guns erupted behind her and pounded the concrete fighting positions of the building beyond. Cale rolled to his left, jumped to his feet, threw a hand grenade, waited for the explosion, and rushed closer toward the building. Casika desperately tried to keep up.

When she finally did reach the next wall, a dozen other Tassian soldiers had already lined up, watching for Cale to send the signal to make the final push. Around her feet lay the bodies of Jark fighters. A few groaned, but none moved. This was the first time she had ever seen a Jark. Even in death their massive red and black corpses frightened her. Jaws the size of her hand lay open; purple tongues hung limp from their mouths.

Peering around the corner, she could see the goal: a bright crystal door, steel and rubble blocking their path. Ten meters, but would they make it? Rounds zipped and popped past her head and vibrated the steel beams she pressed her body against for cover.

"Where are those mortars?" Cale shouted again. "I need their heads down; I need them suppressed!"

Engines roared overhead and Cale once again grabbed Casika and threw her to the ground. A red Jark fighter swooped from above. *This is it,* she thought.

But it wasn't. The gray Mateen warplanes once more swarmed and attacked. The ground shook as the two sides exchanged fire. Missiles exploded and burst. The red plane flamed and smoked. Metal fell from the sky followed by the aircraft and a sickening crunch.

Finally, after what seemed like hours but was in fact only a few minutes, Casika could hear the first mortar explosions. One, then two and three and at last clusters of ten and twenty blanketing the streets and exploding against the doorway and walls of the facility, shattering glass and sending Jark fighters down in their holes to hide from the barrage.

"We aren't stopping at the door for this last dash," Cale ordered his men. "They can see everything through the crystal walls. I don't want to take the chance by stopping again to regroup."

Cale paused to listen to the radio in his ear. "In thirty seconds this barrage is going to end. Karath, when we leave this cover, you clear upward with your platoon. We'll take ground level and head down," Cale ordered. "Don't forget to mark rooms you've cleared!"

Cale raised his left hand to his shoulder and counted "one." On "two," the whole line rocked backward in unison and at the count of "three," they launched forward. The lead man propelled his body over the wall and dashed toward the building. Just as the last mortar landed, Cale and his brave men had pushed past the Jark line and smashed through the broken doors into the building.

Casika remained outside while the raiders raced through the halls. Gunfire echoed against the blackened walls, and smoke enveloped Cale's crew. In the chaos, all Casika could see were muzzle flashes and shadows. Tassian shouting mixed with gunfire, and finally two soldiers exited, dragging a body. It was Karath's. He hadn't even made it to the steps before being cut down by enemy fire.

The platoons fought on and soon they had achieved a foothold and pressed farther in. Casika followed closely behind Cale's men, afraid of being separated but doubting that she was up to the task of this type of fighting.

Lights flickered and small fires simmered as the team descended the stairway, distancing themselves from the sound of gunfire. The plan remained the same. Cale cleared down, and Karath's platoon cleared upward, despite the fact that Karath was no more.

Soon, no fighting could be heard any longer. All was silent except the sparks that flew off of damaged electrical cables. In the darkness,

Casika allowed her imagination to get away from her, and she became more afraid than she had ever been.

Suddenly, an agonized scream as deep as a roar erupted from below. It wasn't Tassian. As the team descended the final steps into the basement of the building, a large Jark stumbled out of the room that had once held the crystal pool. Mysterious silver lights shimmered off his face as he fell to the ground, letting out a grunt and a whimper that tormented Casika with fear and wonder and sorrow for the Jark. Cale rushed to his side to check for weapons and turned him on his stomach as his men tried to restrain him but failed, allowing him to scurry to his feet and stagger towards the stairs.

"Run," the Jark muttered through their translator. "Run."

Casika wanted to heed his advice, but she was paralyzed, not from fear of the warning, but from fear of being the only coward in the group. Suddenly, a hiss filled the stairwell and echoed off of the blackened crystal walls. Casika covered her ears, but the brave Tassian infantrymen rushed inside. Gunfire and screaming followed, along with a noise so terrible she would never forget it. Cale staggered back through the doorway.

"We've got it cornered," he shouted. "I need more firepower!" His last three soldiers rushed into the room. Gathering her courage, Casika entered as well.

Against the far wall of the shimmering silver pools was a forty-foot-long serpent. Its mouth was nearly four meters wide and its fangs foamed with saliva as it writhed from the agony of bullets piercing its thick hide. It writhed, but it didn't fall.

"Keep firing!" Cale shouted. *Didn't he see it wasn't working? Didn't he see the serpent was rising to strike?* In an instant the creature went from being tied to a corner to a full assault, pushing its head forward and snatching two soldiers from the ground with its powerful jaws.

Cale stumbled backward and grabbed his last grenade from his chest, throwing it at the monster that gleefully tore his friends apart.

CHAPTER TWENTY-SEVEN

"Max Thrust," ordered Brokk from the command center of his battleship. Engines roared and the massive Juggernaut lurched as it escaped the Tassian atmosphere towards the battle. On his screen he could see Lago's battleship facing off against two Mateen destroyers and a battleship of their own, but from the opposite side of the planet, Brokk was powerless to intervene.

"Target the closest destroyer," Brokk ordered, sinking into his chair and bringing up the psycho-transmission system so he could connect directly with Lago. So he could level the playing field and coordinate their maneuver as instantaneously as the Mateen horde.

"We're headed your way; three minutes until we're within range. We've got to level the battlefield. Get towards the second sun to increase the magnetic disturbance." Lago nodded inside Brokk's mind and began to pilot his giant ship. Brokk hoped the magnetic field would work; that he could catch them off guard; that he could divide their forces.

"Faster," Brokk ordered. "Get in range. Cut off the pursuit."

"Forty seconds until we're in range," his targeting officer responded.

Forty seconds. Too long. Not soon enough. Lago's battleship was thrusting away from the enemy but the Mateen were pursuing. "Adjust your thrust," Brokk shouted through his mind to Lago. "Throw them off your trail."

"Twenty seconds," roared his targeting officer from his workstation. The deep voiced pure blood Jark slouched over his equipment; green light from his monitors beaming off his face.

Lago's battleship thrusted upward and banked left, narrowly avoiding a depleted neutronium round fired from the pursuing Mateen destroyer. More proximity rounds burst around Lago's vessel as he dipped and veered towards the helium star. Desperate to disrupt the enemies ability to target his ship and to give Brokk time to join the fight.

"Target," Brokk's officer called.

Brokk's Juggernaut finally cleared Tassi and emerged on the far side of the planet just in time to see a Mateen destroyer in pursuit. "Fire," Brokk ordered, feeling the Juggernaut rumble as twenty neutronium rounds erupted from his front facing cannons.

Lasers and explosions suddenly flared from the destroyer, reacting to the new threat but overwhelmed by the sheer quantity of firepower the massive Juggernaut hurled its way. Round after round smashed into its hull, sending the ship splintering and exploding into hundreds of pieces.

"Thrust up," Brokk shouted to his pilot. "We're going to get their attention and come down on top of the battleship. Lago had reached a safe distance from the second sun where the magnetic field was strong and spun his own ship around.

The Juggernaut climbed, angling itself between Lago and the Mateens. Smoke and debris bounced off his hull from the destroyer. Lifeless Mateen bodies floated through the open space. "Target the Mateen battleship," Brokk ordered.

His men acknowledged their command but suddenly his display lit up with enemy warships. "Two more battleships approaching from below," his radar officer shouted. "Hundreds of fighters."

Four against two. An impossible number. Swarming gray Mateen ships coordinating their effort now. Lago saw them too and, with his ship fully turned around, began peppering their approach with munitions. The battleships maneuvered and the rounds fell short. The distance was too great and his element of surprise had disappeared. Like a swarm of insects, an innumerable amount of sleek gray fighters rushed from the bays of the attacking battleships, swooping and swarming, complicating Brokk's defenses.

"Incoming," shouted his radar officer. The pilot pressed hard on their engines and thrust the Juggernaut down. Explosions rocked his ship above. Computers and sensors flickered. *Too close,* Brokk thought, and then to Lago, "We won't survive this, we've got to get out of here."

Thoughts flooded back over his psycho-transmission device. *Doubt, fear, worry;* not for himself but for Brokk. Finally a response. "You go. I'll cover your withdrawal. Give you time to collect the remaining troops on the planet."

"You'll die," Brokk responded. "We'll fight this together." But the response through Lago's thoughts was strong and resolute. *He would do it alone. Hope. A chance maybe. And then a lie. He was hiding something. His ship had been damaged. Escape was impossible. He couldn't complete a wormhole jump. Surrender was out of the question.*

"Get us back into orbit," Brokk ordered. "Evacuate whoever is left; collect their shuttles as we cross the planet."

Lago's ship charged as Brokk escaped the battle and the sun. Proximity rounds and munitions burst everywhere, each side swarming and attacking as the lone Jark battleship rushed into the fray.

Suddenly, the fear that poured through his mental communication device stopped and sharp pain flooded across the void of space and into Brokk's mind. Grabbing his forehead, he screamed as Lago's pain filled him to the brim. He could see it all. A dense neutronium round fired from the battleship tore through the bridge of his ship. As air rushed from Lago's lungs, his body depressurized, squeezed, and finally popped.

Brokk couldn't take it anymore and slung himself to the ground, ripping the device from his head. "Lago!" he screamed bitterly at the crew that surrounded him. *Lago.*

The final moments of his dear friend's life were forever carved into his mind in the worst way imaginable. He felt his fear in battle and his agony in death. Brokk couldn't handle it, but the thought of another name suddenly crept into his mind and as a fire extinguisher suffocates flames, so too did hatred and revenge replace his anguish. *Gemini.*

Gemini did this. *Gemini.*

***

The black serpent rose above Cale and Casika, stunned for a moment from the grenade and lashing its tail back and forth in anguish. The grenade had hurt the beast but not enough. Out of ammo, all that remained between them was the pale silver mercury from which the grootslang had been summoned.

Hissing, it struck at Casika from across the pool. She dove to her right and its head smashed into the far wall, causing bricks and concrete to fall and sunlight to pour in from the outside. "Casika," Cale shouted. "There's an exit. Keep running, I'll distract it!"

Struggling to get to her feet, pain shot from her legs and into her chest. Blackness crept into her vision, but she wouldn't pass out. She couldn't. *Fight on. Don't give in.* Clenching her teeth, Casika pressed onward. Rolling closer to the mercury pool, she pushed herself up on her elbows, but something seized her. A hand. Two. Filthy hair covered hands coated in silver slime reached up from the pool and tried to drag her down. Clawing at her pants and her feet. Slippery slime covered hands gripping her bare calf and tugging at her ankle. "Help!" she cried out, but her cries tightened their grip. They wanted her. *Needed her. Creatures from another world; from a nightmare that yearned to feel the warmth of her life and taste the heat of her flesh.*

"Get up, Casika," Cale shouted, running to her side and grabbing her arms to pull against the hands in the pool. "Get up! We have to!"

he cried as he struggled to pull her free.

The snake hissed and rose again, poising for another strike. It would get them both now. Cale gripped Casika's arm and threw his body over her face. Just as it began to lower its head, the beast let out a cry and writhed in agony. Cale turned and Casika struggled to focus in the dark, but suddenly it was clear what happened. Arden, her Mateen protector, had leapt from an alcove above onto the snake's head and was shoving a two-foot-long Mateen battle knife into its skull.

"Get out," he roared from above, driving the blade deeper into the beast's scaly head. It twisted and spun, lurched upwards and surged back, desperate to get the brave Mateen off, but it was no use. Arden's arms held and as he inched the blade deeper into the innards of the creature, the snake's strength surged, shooting itself straight up into the ceiling. Bricks and dust fell and suddenly Arden was falling too. The mighty Mateen, dethroned from his position dropped limply into the mercury pool below.

"Arden!" Casika shouted. Hands loosed their grip and slithered off her pants, descending downward into their silver grave. There was something else in the pool that now caught their attention. *Arden.* Casika was free.

In the subsequent silence, Casika and Cale waited for a time, hoping someone would rise from the depths, but no one did. Blue light shone through a massive hole in the building. The beast had escaped; but Casika didn't care. Her strength had failed her. Her whole body shook. *Terrified. Petrified. Frozen. Heart-broken. Arden.*

"How deep do you think that pool is?" Casika finally asked Cale who looked helplessly into the pool.

"I've swam in it before," Cale responded. "Three feet at most."

"He's still in there. We have to get him." Casika insisted.

Cale rose to his feet and fixed his eyes on the pool. No bubbles floated to the surface and the mercury remained still and unmoving. His body did not float. *Impossible.*

Cale reached out his hand and helped Casika to her feet. "He's dead," he responded frankly. How can we go in there? We know what's waiting."

Casika had no answer; only sorrow. "We owe him more than that," she muttered. *But how.* Cale was right. Arden was dead.

Supporting each other's weight, the two Tassians climbed the stairwell and exited the shrouded government building in silence. Soldiers and citizens mingled together on the streets, staring at a giant black lump of flesh and scale. It lay motionless. Dead from the Mateen blade that was still lodged in its head.

"What is it?" she heard a soldier ask.

"A gift from the Jarks," Cale responded addressing the crowd. "Don't ever forget what they've left us!"

On the roof above, Cale and Casika could see the rest of their company. A crowd was gathering to watch the soldiers on the roof cut the ropes that held the black cloth against their crystal building. As the drapes fell, the crowd was silenced. Their beautiful crystal building sparkled with a glory Casika had never remembered seeing before.

"Why did they cover the building?" she asked Cale.

"So no one could see the evil they planned inside," he responded.

"Out of sight, out of mind, I suppose."

Casika wasn't convinced, but before she could mull on it further, Gemini's dark gray battleship crested the horizon and hovered off the gulf. In the sunlight, the Mateen battleship was more magnificent that she could ever dream. It was over. The battle for their planet had ended.

BEYOND THE JUMP

Shoulder to shoulder, Gemini and Casika walked silently through the thick forest of Rodam. Any breeze had been long smothered by the thick canopy of orange-barked trees that coated the moon's surface. Sweat poured off his face, but the gray-skinned warrior kept his pace. Casika could tell that Gemini was deep in thought, collective thought, the type that had caused her to grow so fond of the Mateens and their mysterious ways.

Finally, the two reached a clearing in the trees, and he stopped before slowly walking out onto the rock ledge beyond. She was grateful for the break, but even more so for the breeze that now pressed against her face and cooled her body from the arduous hike. Before her was a rock that jutted out over a green-and-orange valley below. "It's beautiful," she said at last. "This is the perfect place for him."

Gemini said nothing but gave her an approving look. During their ordeal, Casika had learned how to understand his facial expressions, and she knew that he was deeply hurt by the loss of his friend. More so, she suspected his grief for Arden would have been overwhelming if not for the help of the collective that, like a great cloud, embraced one another in love, mercy, and compassion during their hardships.

Gemini moved to the edge of the cliff and sat, placing his elbows on his knees. Casika followed and found a place to sit with him. After a moment more of silence, he pointed to the horizon in the darkening sky. "We'll see him pass by right over there," he finally said.

Casika watched a moment longer, and then, like a meteor entering the atmosphere, an orange-and-yellow streak fell from the sky. "There he goes," she said, giving Gemini a timid smile. "Were you with him when he died?" she asked.

"We all were," he responded, still watching the horizon. "We all were."

"Was he scared?"

"No, we were with him. He was at peace."

"Even to the end?"

"Even to the end." Gemini responded.

Casika knew he didn't feel like talking, but she also felt drawn to press him with more questions. She wasn't part of the collective and desperately needed to make sense of her own experience. "And the pool?" she asked, "You really didn't find anything?"

"Nothing," he responded. "When we drained it, we only found Arden, lungs full of mercury. No people. No hands. Just Arden."

"I don't understand…" She trailed off. Gemini didn't say anything. If he was with Arden, he knew the truth to her story, and that was enough for her, even if he didn't understand it either. "What is going to happen now? You know, between the Jarks and the rest of us?"

"I'm not sure. But I'll leave the politics to our politicians. Brokk hasn't been seen since by anyone. The Jarks insisted he was acting out of line, that he had gone rogue against the wishes of their government. They've declared him a war criminal."

For the first time since they'd arrived on Rodam, Gemini looked at her and gave an expression she longed to see—one of doubt. This was the same expression he had given her when she had told her own story in his office so long ago.

Casika raised her eyebrows. "Wow. Is that true?"

"I don't know," he responded. "If we find him, we'll bring him to justice and learn the truth. If not, he's powerless to do any more damage anyway. The Jarks are embarrassed, and that will keep them from their imperialism for a time." Gemini paused and shifted his gaze from her back to the horizon to watch the dozens of other bodies lost in the battle sail to their planet below. After a moment he fixed his eyes on her again. "How's Cale?"

"Shaken, saddened, bewildered."

Gemini was silent for some time and then made a point to stare her in the eyes "Cale is a good man, Casika."

She laughed. "I ran away from home when my mother started down that road."

Gemini didn't smile, but she could read his expressions better now and she knew what he was thinking. "He's a good man," he repeated, "and that's all I'll say about it."

***

In a dark, red-lit room, Brokk sat motionless, looking out the window of his battleship and into the airless void beyond. Try as he might, he could never escape the death that he felt Lago experience from the space outside that window. In the distance, a reddish haze could be seen as sunlight from a nearby star illuminated a dwarf planet. It was a small planet that orbited a small star, but this was an outlaw's paradise and the perfect place to find refuge while he rebuilt his fleet and considered his next move.

Lost as he was in his thoughts, the metallic creak of his cabin door thrust him into the present. Turning, Brokk locked eyes with his shackled prisoner, captured in the final battle. A Jark officer pushed the weary man forward and grabbed the chain that wrapped around his hands to jerk him upright. "Good of you to make it, Remmel," Brokk said, standing to greet him. "I wonder what they pay for Tassians down there."

End of Book One

ACKNOWLEDGMENTS

A big thank you to Sarah Keller for the beautiful book design. Thank you to Sarah Keller, Andrea Keller, James Griffes, and Tom Lasch for taking time to read through and critique my work - over and over again.

Thanks to all of my readers, especially those that that take the time to review my work on Amazon and Goodreads. I read through every review posted and I'm eternally grateful for the opportunity I get to correspond with my fans.

ABOUT THE AUTHOR

Thane is a graduate of the Virginia Military Institute with a degree in psychology and a minor in English. Following college, Thane married his high school sweetheart Sarah and started his career as a cavalryman in the United States Army. Over the course of his career, he has deployed to both Iraq and Afghanistan where he was personally engaged in ground combat. His service has thus far earned him two Bronze Stars and numerous other awards and decorations.

Relying on his psychology background, military experience, and Christian faith, Thane writes novels that seek to explore human nature under dire circumstances, the reality of pain and suffering, and the resilience of individuals to accomplish superhuman feats. Thane's hopes are that as readers experience his character's journey through the gift of reading, they will be greater equipped to endure the inevitable ups and downs in life itself and dream to accomplish grander things.

In addition to his wife Sarah, Thane is blessed to have four wonderful children that do all they can to keep him from pursuing his love of writing.

PREVIEW THE NOVEL: ROGUE FLEET

What's next for Brokk and his exiled crew? Preview Rogue Fleet below!

Available on Amazon and at your local book stores

BEFORE THE JUMP

"Look alive," called a red-headed, barrel-chested man wearing a gray tank top that used to be white. Red, a name he had picked up because of his fire red hair and pale white skin, sent shivers up the spine of anyone that dared to cross him. He was good at his job and he commanded his vessel with an iron fist. He kept them alive too, but when mercenaries complained about their leader they rarely considered the good. "We're crossing the border zone!" he bellowed, wandering from station to station to ensure his men were scanning their sector.

Three of them, one at the front and one on each side manned laser cannons that supposedly cut a ship in half in a matter of seconds if someone crossed him. None ever had but Tamara wasn't sad that she didn't get to see the show. It was a far better strategy to let a mercenary boast about the capabilities of his ship rather than be forced to show her what it could do in a dogfight.

Tamara glanced over at Red and smiled. She liked him. She always had. Red grabbed his handle bar mustache and gave her a wink, his pale white skin shining whiter than ever under the florescent lights in the cabin of the transport ship. He fancied himself more desirable than he really was. Another aspect of his shining personality.

"You gonna keep us safe up here, Red?" She asked.

Red stood for a moment and stared at her, rubbing his mustache the whole time. She suspected he wanted to say something deep and meaningful, but that just wasn't Red. The deeper he thought, the harder he rubbed his face until finally Red's foot, covered in a black leather boot, started tapping too. Somehow that mustache must have been hardwired into his brain because when he rubbed the hair on his mustache, the foot couldn't help but stomp. Finally, after what would be an awkward length of time for anyone else, Red conceded and threw the question back at her. "I should ask you the same thing."

"You know I don't work well up here in the void. Not much oxygen, Red." She looked around the cabin and out of the window before adding "not many elements to play with either."

"Yeah, yeah, I know. None of us want to die if you get out of sorts," he responded with a bit of disappointment in his deep brown eyes. "I had to ask though."

The burly man flexed his chest as he walked past Tamara and continued his checks in the cabin of the small vessel. Their trip was a relatively small one, only fifty parsecs to travel, or the equivalent distance between the planet Hestos and the moon of Charlon. Their ship, a small transport vessel carrying about sixty passengers, four marines, two pilots, and Tamara was a trading ship but had recently been contracted to supply workers to the ever-growing farming requirements on Charlon. The folks they carried were happy for the work and Tamara was happy for some fresh air away from the bustle of Hestos.

As they entered the border zone, their ship groaned and creaked. Tamara could see the steel bulkheads pressing inward but she knew they would hold. They always did. Gravity was distorted in the border zone and pressed on even the most well-constructed vessel in ways that nobody could guess. Not anybody on this ship at least.

As the ship entered, the once blackness of space was suddenly a soup of colors bombarding the small portholes evenly spaced in the crew compartment. Reds, yellows, greens, and blues penetrated every crack of the ship forcing the gray bulkheads and silver floors to reflect a magical array of rainbows throughout the cabin. There were more elements now, but still nowhere to run if she allowed herself to be tempted, if she allowed herself to reach out and seize the boiling gasses of the Rainbow Nebula. No, deep space and the center of a nebula were no place for her talents.

Suddenly Tamara heard laughing from the front of the cabin and saw a small Hestonian boy, no older than thirteen giggling and pointing. "His hair is purple, like a girls!" the boy exclaimed gleefully. Tamara found the source of their entertainment just in time to see Red storming out of the passenger cabin and towards his pilots. Suddenly, she realized his hair was purple from the blue light of the nebula inundating is features. Even his mustache was purple and hid the scowl of contempt he held for the workers that mocked him.

So space can humble even the most barbaric of men, she thought to herself, giggling a bit but suddenly feeling terrible for the man that was so easily angered. He wasn't a bad man, but he was demanding to work for and he relied far too readily on the false image that he sought to portray. Empathy was her strength and she felt it more for Red than she did anyone else. As a young girl, it was him and his team of mercenaries that saw worth in her. Where on Hestos, a place of logic and science she was an outcast, he took her in and made her his own. She clung to him like a father. *And what child isn't just a little embarrassed for their father?*

Tamara wasn't a marine, but she was a fighter and her worth to Red was more than just the company of a daughter. Tamara was a half-breed, a mix of Lysop and Hestonian that gave her certain gifts. Men who didn't understand feared her people, but those who did, men like Red, knew there was nothing mythical or magical about the things she could do; she simply had a greater understanding of nature. A greater sense of the form that elements took and the properties of those elements under certain conditions. That understanding gave her the chance to manipulate the natural world and create things entirely out of the ordinary.

Call her a witch or a wizard and you might be right, but Tamara didn't think so. To her, it was as natural as talking and as enjoyable too. There were constraints of course, but as she grew under his tutelage she learned to harness her understanding and had only once mistakenly seared his fire-red hair.

"Hit the thrusters!" She heard Red shout from the cockpit. Instantly, pressure increased on her chest as the ship pushed against the soupy nebula that exerted its own force against the small gray vessel. "Is that all you've got?" He shouted again, chastising the pilots for the lack of power in the nebula. "My mother can swim faster than this!"

He wasn't simply bellowing orders, however. Underneath the humor and the insults, Tamara suddenly sensed panic in his voice and climbed to her feet to rush towards the open cockpit.

"What is it?" she asked, reaching him as he left.

He ignored her, instead searching for his marines. "Lock and load, we've got pirates coming!" he hollered.

Gasps filled the cabin and scared passengers looked towards their fearless red-haired leader for guidance. The smile that once rested smugly on the young boy's face was now flat and fearful; his eyes wide with dread.

"What about the lasers?" She asked, watching as the men manning the guns pushed away and grabbed their personal rifles.

"Won't work in here," was his response. "Too dense, we'd ignite the whole cloud. Want to die?" he asked, looking at her before turning his attention to his men. "Jakk, put their heads down and take position behind that steel," he ordered. Tamara looked to see a man with hair as dark as coal and a black beard moving through the cabin with a rifle held high. He looked calm, but she could hear his heart beating fast in his chest. She could sense the blood pulsing beneath his veins supplying nutrients and adrenaline to his muscles.

The border zone was no place to get caught by pirates and made for an impossible rescue. If the enemy vessel breached their hull they would be burned alive by the scalding nebula. If their engines were damaged, they would sink to the core of the gaseous beast until all of their food and life support had been depleted and the gravity of the nebula itself crushed them all to death. Their only chance was to run to open space and hope they had enough power left to escape the pursuing ships.

Suddenly, Tamara felt thrusters fire, this time pressing upward on their bodies. The pilots were trying to evade the pursuing vessel and seek a way out of the cloud. Immense pressure attacked her lungs. Her breathing was short and her vision faded.

The cloud was too dense, too deep, and too thick to think. Colors continued to pour in through the window at a dizzying rate of speed. Green. Yellow. Blue. Red. Green. Orange. Then nothing. Blackness. They had escaped. The pressure on her chest disappeared. Sighs of relief filled the cabin but a jolt and a shriek brought Tamara back to reality.

A small spear the size of her fist ripped through the steel hull of their ship and anchored like a grappling hook into the rear wall. Oxygen rushed from the vessel but a second jolt pulled the hook tight against the frame and sealed the hole.

"They've got us!" shouted Red. "Suit up! Get your oxygen masks on!"

Panic ensued as frenzied passengers gripped for their belongings, desperately searching for their emergency kits in the event of a damaged hull or other disaster. Tamara too zipped her blue jumpsuit up to her throat and pulled a hooded mask up from behind. She could feel oxygen fill the suit, but there was something else as well. Complete silence. The ships engines had been dampened. They were fully in the grip of the enemy ship. Lights flickered and faded, replaced with the red emergency lights that came on when they were operating on auxiliary power, fueled by the batteries that contained who knew how many hours of life support before they were done for.

Tamara sensed Red's approach and spun around to see that he too had switched out his filthy tank top for a clean black jumpsuit. A clear mask covered his eyes and mouth. At first, he didn't speak, instead looking at her figure in her skin-tight space suit. In the midst of panic, Red always found a way to show people he simply didn't care. His interest in the carnal was paramount at all times and never once wavered in the realm of uncertainty.

"I can still make your blood boil from inside your suit," Tamara said.

"My blood is boiling just looking at you, girl," was his response. She didn't retort and he didn't give her the time to. "Can you sense anything up there?" He asked, suddenly with fearful dread coating his words. "Are you connected to them by the harpoon cable?"

Tamara tried, but she couldn't. "The void... they're too far still," she strained.

"It's okay, girl." He responded. "They'll be here soon, maybe you can feel them then."

He never accused her, never demanded anything of her. He was her comfort and her rock. He cared for her unconditionally, even in this moment where she felt helpless and desperate. At a time where she should be panicked and considering the past and her future and what might become of her, she instead looked up to the calmness of her captain and found peace.

The ship creaked and jolted as the larger vessel reeled them in like fish caught in the sea. The groaning of steel being pushed and contorted intensified until a sickening realization struck Tamara—they had docked. The enemy ship was directly above them. Suddenly, pounding could be heard and the pale shrieks of steel yielding to cutters filled the compartment. Marines fixed their weapons on the ceiling, waiting to extinguish the threat.

They wouldn't get their chance. The enemy was prepared. As soon as the ceiling of the ship had been cut, they simply let the ten-ton steel object fall into the cabin below. Passengers screamed as smoke filled the compartment. Guns erupted upwards shooting at anything that dared enter, but it was too late. The filter on her suit was never calibrated to remove the toxin emitted from the smoke grenades that now filled her lungs.

Losing control of her body, Tamara fell hard to the ground. As her vision faded she could see Red standing tall, firing his weapon. Then everything was black.

CHAPTER ONE

Fluffy white clouds drifted across a deep blue sky. The sun peaked out just long enough to expose the hundreds of workers below to its warmth and then dipped behind another meandering monster. It was midday and Tamara was starving, but she had not yet reached her quota and lunch was served proportionately to the amount of fruit an individual picked.

A breeze pushed inland from the south, carrying with it the scent of salt from an inland sea and kicking up dust into the faces of the slaves that labored against the elements for a few good greltins. The small bulbous fruit typically grew in clusters on tall orange vines but the drought had been vicious this year and Tamara and her companions were worked even harder to get every last ounce they could scavenge before the harvest season ended.

Tamara stepped through a series of wires holding the greltin vines to the wooden posts and examined the next section. They were bare. A second gust of wind hurled more dust into her face from the south and she grimaced, tucking her hazel green eyes deeper into the cloth that covered her mouth and nose.

The protective tuck brought a sharp pain to her skull and reminded her not to move too quickly. Even after five years, the metal crown she wore that was screwed into her skull at the corners of her head to stop her from escaping still hurt if she moved too quickly.

"It looks like we might finally get some rain," whispered a fellow slave over her shoulder. "Keep some of that dust down."

Tamara agreed but declined to respond and hated him for risking the attention of the overseer for such an obvious comment. As the other man worked, he eventually passed her by without another word. Feeling her hot breath venting up into her eyes, Tamara turned from the wind and dropped the cloth down to her neck, eager to breathe the unfiltered air.

It was a hot day, but not the hottest of days. She was grateful for the clouds to block the sun but dreamed of the mountains beyond their dusty farm on the outskirts of their town. The mountains, like an oasis in the desert, shot up from the north against the backdrop of a dust-filled horizon. More attractive than the mystery of the wild was their rich green color that promised clear water and dust free air. In the evenings after a long day's work, Tamara listened to slave tales of rivers flowing abundantly and more food than anyone could hope to eat.

It was nearly every day that Tamara considered escaping there, but she couldn't; not because of fear but because of the nagging question—*what then?* She wouldn't survive long with the crown blocking out her mind; certainly not if she was confronted by a pack of wild animals. In truth, she knew she was without options, and while she vaguely remembered the life she once lived, it was simply a memory, a ghost from the past, an inconsequential cluster of neurons that distracted her from her work.

Tamara turned back to the greltin vines just in time to notice the overseer was watching her. She had allowed her eyes to linger on the mountains too long and now her taskmaster had become suspicious.

Moving quickly from vine to vine, Tamara tried to look busy in her work, but he had already come down from his stoop and was walking towards her. Panic surged from within. A pit grew in her stomach and erupted upward towards her throat.

Tamara walked quickly to the next row, desperate to pass his gaze. Hopeful that he would see something else that dissatisfied him and forget about her. It didn't work and his hot breath was soon heavy on the back of her neck as he leaned in to spin her around.

The stench of garlic and onions carried a raspy voice with it. "What were you looking at, girl?" he asked, every word dripping with indignation and hatred for the slave he was forced to watch over.

Tamara tried to look innocent. She tried to speak but the pit that had moved to her throat clogged the words. She swallowed and tried again. "The vines," she said. "I'm searching for clusters of greltin."

He held her gaze for a moment, penetrating his brown eyes deep into hers. His leathered skin, darkened from years of laboring in the sun, glistened with fresh sweat that had drained from gaps in his dusty brown tunic. It was a heavy cloth for this time of year, burlap and cotton, catching the heat of the sun and torturing its wearer. Tamara's eyes darted over his large body. The burlap was tied at the waist with a leather belt. Attached to the belt and hanging off one hip was a whip, which he now reached for.

"I swear," she murmured. "I swear I wasn't looking at anything. Please believe me, I swear." She raised her hand to her face as he lifted his own to slap her, but instead, the large dark-haired man grabbed her by the wrist and threw her to the ground.

Dust splashed up as she sunk into the heavily traveled soil and her head rung in agony from the jostling of her slave collar that had been bolted into her skull. He would have known the pain such a throw would cause as he too held the scars of a former slave on his forehead; marks of a man who came from humble roots but now found his calling torturing those that were not as fortunate to buy their own freedom.

Tamara tried to scramble to her feet but her overseer had already unlatched his whip and rose it above his head to discipline the helpless woman. The first snap struck her forearm and she screamed in pain. Her vision blurred as tears welled in her eyes but she fought them from pouring to the surface, feeling a cold wet trickle of blood drain from her arm and drip to the dirt below. The whip sunk into flesh a second time, sending shooting pain up her back as she curled to protect herself.

From the corner of her eye, she could see him raise his arm for a third strike but stopped. In the distance, a voice called the cruel man to a halt and she recognized it. Her master. Her owner. Temporarily her protector. *Temporarily.* "Send her to me," the man shouted.

The overseer reached down and grabbed her arm, pulling her to her feet like she was a child throwing a tantrum. Dust kicked up against her open flesh as he drug her upwards, stinging the raw wound. Through tear-blurred eyes she could see her *temporary* savior clothed in white standing on the balcony of his stone villa, disappearing as he walked inside, but his status as savior wouldn't last. She knew it wouldn't. She had been there before, summoned by the one that owned her body and she instantly regretted ever looking at those mountains.

"Take my word for it, girl," the overseer said dragging her towards the villa. "You don't want anything to do with those mountains. If the cold doesn't get you, the beasts will. It's untamed; even the strongest warriors don't last more than a day." He looked her up and down as they walked before adding. "You wouldn't last more than a few hours."

Tamara didn't respond. Anything she said would surely earn her additional punishment. As the brute brought her closer to her master's house, she knew the night would bring greater pains than this man's aggression could have brought in a lifetime of beating. Where the overseer could only force the whip, her master owned her. All of her.

Tonight, he would make her wish she had never distracted him from his work and in the morning, try as she might to hate him, she would be forced to make amends for her captors and look forward to another day. If she didn't... if she refused to forgive them, the guilt and hatred would surely overcome her. Then where would she be? Depressed? Suicidal? No, Tamara would bide her time and keep herself healthy and one day, like the overseer that hit her, she might be free.

"When you get inside, you only refer to him as Master or Lord. Do you understand?" he growled, stopping to face her.

She nodded. "Yes, overseer."

"Good."

They had reached a brown front door made of darkened wood and bolted to the tan sandstone exterior. Two older women, the master's servants, waited in the lobby wearing tan burlap aprons stained from food and dust. Their dark hair was pulled back into a bun and at once they rushed out to grab the slave from the overseer's hands.

"Come," one of the women said. "Let's get you cleaned up so you are presentable to Master Orno. You remember how particular he is?" she asked, looking Tamara up and down before finally gasping in despair. "This just will not do," she said in a high-pitched squeal. "Jelna, get the medical kit, we've got to have her healed up. He won't like this at all, no, no, no," the woman muttered with an outstretched hand, gesturing for Tamara's.

Tamara accepted and suddenly the warm calloused hand of the housemaid had gripped her and was pulling her quickly through the home. It had only been a few months since her last encounter but the home had already been renovated. Sandstone tile was replaced with creamy marble and the light stone staircase that led up to the main dining hall had been cleaned and painted. Pots full of plants lined the hallways and the smell of flowers nearly overwhelmed her.

Despite the many changes, this was the same old villa and tortured memories of agonized nights fluttered back into her mind, tormenting her. The pit in her stomach that she so eagerly fought back down with the overseer outside suddenly ballooned upwards again and into her throat. Desperation engulfed her and she felt as if she would explode in nervous anxiety. Her face was hot and cold at the same time and each step, forced by the short fat woman felt weak under the weight of her body.

Fighting down the urge to throw up and pass out she tried to focus her mind elsewhere. It was hard with the collar and even the walls refused her ability to sense their texture. Her life was dark and without feeling, trapped within the fleshy walls of her skin, bones, and organs. Finally, upon passing a window at the back of the home, she set her mind to the mountain and all the solitude that it offered her. She *would* escape but first she had to survive. This was going to be a long night.

CHAPTER TWO

"A planet that doesn't rotate?" Brokk was on the bridge of his battleship receiving a brief from his staff. After narrowly escaping Tassi, they had arrived to Charoth, a planet of outlaws where he would rebuild his fleet and hopefully restock his crew. It was a big task that lay ahead of the now hunted battleship and her leader. He hoped they could succeed, but since Lago's death, doubt continually surfaced to the forefront of his thoughts.

"Yes, Commander," his pilot Terre responded. "The side we are currently facing is deathly cold and never exposed to the sun, but because of the planet's location and distance, the sun-facing side is able to maintain plenty of warmth without the overbearing effects on its plant and animal life."

"So this is why it's able to evade the prying eyes of our governments," Brokk thought out loud.

"Exactly. Charoth shouldn't exist. When scientists search for habitable planets, they look for ones that rotate because that is how a planet maintains its magnetic field, maintains its climate, and maintains its atmosphere. This one is truly an anomaly; making it the perfect place for us to regain our strength."

Brokk knew the last line wasn't a dig, but it still hurt. The scars of losing Lago and the Battle for Tassi were only a few weeks old and he could still taste the bitterness of their defeat fresh in his mouth. Defeat he could deal with, betrayal however, betrayal stung almost as bad as the loss of his best friend. His blood still boiled from the anger and an animalistic rage that brewed beneath his skin.

Brokk had been abandoned by his people and made to look like a fool in front of the Galactic Order. This very morning, Brokk woke to a nightmare, reliving Lago's death over and over again as if it was his own. He felt the bitter cold grip him, oxygen rush from his lungs. He would wake up gagging; gasping for the oxygen that he knew existed but was too distant to breathe. Try as he might, he couldn't get Lago's death out of his head. It was changing him, tormenting him, destroying him. Lago's death was his own near-death experience and for a reason he could not fathom, it terrified him beyond his limits.

Some days, Brokk wished it had been his own life that was sucked out into the abyss. His own eyes that exploded from the sudden change of pressure by being ripped into space. Lago would have dealt with this defeat far better, but it was Brokk who was left alive and for whatever the reason, he determined in his mind seize the opportunity to repay betrayal for betrayal, blood for blood, and death for death.

His crew waited patiently and Brokk suddenly realized he had been stewing for too long. He had done this a lot lately and Brokk worried that the men he led were beginning to notice. *Focus.* "How does it maintain those essential qualities with no rotation?"

Terre smiled. "I'm going to do a terrible job quoting our scientists, but what they tell me is that the planet is actually leaching a magnetic field from the nebula it orbits so closely to. In fact, it's likely that the star and the planet both were born to the nebula and are only recently drifting to a safe orbit where life can exist."

Brokk shrugged. "Whatever you say, Terre. Have you found us a place to land our ship?"

"We have," his top pilot answered, spinning a three-dimensional hologram of the planet until he had found the location he wanted. Zooming in, Terre pointed to a plot of farms near the mountains that divided the frozen wasteland from the habitable portion of the planet.

"Obviously, landing your battleship here is ill-advised, but we think building a base camp near this mountain range is a great option. We can keep the battleship functioning from above, using its scanners to search for threats while we conduct our operations from the surface. Our probes reveal the mountain itself is capable of sustaining a small outpost while you explore the city. If our food replication fails, there is wild game to hunt and grains and fruit in abundance."

Terre stepped back and allowed Brokk to examine the map more fully. Terre was full blood Jark but had perfected the ability to stand upright without slouching. His large frame and jet black hair complimented the confidence that he exhibited in his work. To be a fighter pilot, you had to be at the top of your game. To earn the title of Top Pilot, you had to be nothing short of remarkable.

"How far is it from the city and the main spaceport? We'll want to trade and hire crew to replace the ones we lost. I want to survey the ships and build a new fleet of planetary fighters to fill my empty hangars. Can I do all of that from the outpost?"

"I think you can. Even amongst outlaws, word travels fast. We don't want anyone saying Brokk and his fleet of renegades are here," Terre said with a chuckle through a mouthful of razor-sharp teeth. "Piracy is the main economy; we risk someone spilling information you want hidden if we take up residence near the port. Besides," Terre added, "the mountains are dark and shaded. We don't want to relive the constant sunlight from Tassi."

Another dig but Brokk let it pass. They had learned more than one lesson from Tassi. His crew had changed. Brokk had changed. They would dust themselves off and they would learn. If that meant a few misplaced insults had to be absorbed to avoid reliving past mistakes, Brokk would be happy to shoulder them. "Very well. Let's make it happen. Keep the Juggernaut on the far side of the planet. I'll take a shuttle with a company of marines while a second shuttle begins constructing the camp. Ensure we have sufficient defenses, to include ground to air. No mistakes; keep our fortress solid. Remember that we're in hostile territory. These aren't trained soldiers but they're gang leaders and mobsters with a business to run. They'll see us as a threat if we slip up before we're ready to take over."

Terre nodded and prepared to continue but Brokk wasn't ready and instead raised his finger for silence. "And who benefits from the trade?" Brokk asked, certain he knew the answer but eager to let his crew hear it from an unbiased mouth.

Terre hesitated to answer but seeing Brokk's silence he finally conceded. "The Jark Empire seems to benefit from most of the slavery. There are some Hestonian traders that buy slaves as well."

Brokk rubbed his chin but remained silent, letting the information soak in. Finally, after a few more moments Brokk addressed the group as a whole. "The same empire that betrayed us; that left us for dead after sending us to conquer the Tassians has been dealing in the slave trade and drug smuggling. We were trained in the honor of our ancestors," he scoffed, "this is a disgrace." He paused to let his speech soak in before making one final statement. "We already have operatives in the capital. The government is called the Iralene; they are merely a shadow government for the Jark Empire. Remember this. We strike the Iralene, we strike our betrayers."

Brokk spun the hologram around and zoomed in closer on one of the larger farms. While the landscape was speckled with homes, this one was larger than the others and had three other large structures that could house people hostile to his cause. "I want to see who's living on those farms. We're going to need to come to an agreement with them first. We don't need anyone alerting the city that there is a new group in town." He paused again choosing his next words carefully and making sure to address his entire staff. "We can't afford any mistakes. Our mind has to be on the goal. Everyone is our enemy. Everyone."

Brokk looked over to the chief of his army, a man who had served him honorably time and time again. On Tassi, he almost paid with his life. The scarred pure blood Jark, a thick-faced, red-skinned man, breathed heavily as he absorbed the map with his eyes and committed it to memory.

Of the two eyes that he started life with only one now remained; the other was missing completely, leaving only a stitched over flap of skin to remind everyone of his sacrifice. His left arm too rested higher than his right as a result of a broken shoulder that was still healing. Long black and silver hair contrasted sharply with his red skin and, noticing Brokk was staring, he rose to his feet.

"We will of course be ready, Commander."

"I know you will, Canis." Brokk said warmly, then deciding to add, "I'm glad to see you on your feet again. I've been hoping for your full recovery."

Canis didn't smile but instead took his seat again and returned his gaze to the holographic map. With the blue light from the hologram beaming against his face, Brokk could see the full extent of his injuries. Wide gashes covered his cheeks and forehead from his battle with the grootslang. On his temple was a puncture wound, starting above his ear and jutting backward from where a fang narrowly missed penetrating his skull.

Canis had been lucky; but upon learning of his attempted sacrifice, Brokk went into a fury. He gleefully executed the priests that survived the Mateen counter-attack, not just for Canis, but for Lago as well. The priests wrongly read and accepted the infant sacrifice as a symbol that the dead would give them victory. The dead did not, and in turn, Brokk executed their messengers. He decided he was done with their false religion. If the dead had no power in this world as indicated by their defeat and if the priests had no ability to discern that, he would either find new gods or abandon them altogether.

Now, they would rebuild and as his staff examined the map and made notes based on his instructions, Brokk went through his list again. The first order of business was to learn about Charoth, a planet of outlaws and vagrants. With the current information, Brokk believed that the fastest way to grow the fleet was to seize a sizable amount of illicit operations. If ships were being pirated he wanted to intercept the goods. If slaves were being sold, he wanted the first cut so the skilled wouldn't go to waste. If people were being killed, he would find a way to spin it against the current government. Brokk needed to put his hand in everything on this worthless planet, and then, when he was good and ready, he would make the Jark Empire pay for their betrayal until he had executed their king himself.

Climbing to his feet, the men in the command center of his ship snapped to attention. "I'll be ready in twenty minutes, Canis. I'll meet you at the launch bay."

Without waiting for a response, Brokk left the command center and walked down the main corridor towards his private quarters. He went to Tassi to be a chancellor and was betrayed. He would go to Charoth as a warlord and there would be no mercy for those that crossed him.

The three-minute walk from his command post to his quarters gave him enough time to switch mental gears. Remmel, the captured general from Tassi, waited outside the door with his hands and feet shackled. Two Jark guards bracketed him on each side. The pale-skinned general stood taller than his men, but he was frail and old. Wrinkles covered his worried face and his hair had grown long during the three weeks of imprisonment. The gray mop of hair on top of his head now draped over his forehead and rested messily on his shoulders.

He looked weak, but Brokk knew he was well fed. Brokk also knew not to trust appearances. This was the same man that confessed to killing his own kind just to survive. Brokk knew Remmel was a cutthroat leader and he wouldn't dare let his guard down around the man.

"We've stopped," the old man said spitefully, looking him in the eyes with indignation he had only gotten once before from the Tassian chancellor.

"Today is your lucky day," responded Brokk. "I'm going to sell you at the market down there." He paused to make a show of looking the man that hated him so much up and down. Brokk knew his fleet's defeat brought great joy to Remmel; he didn't want the man to see that it affected him at all. "I wonder if anyone will even buy an old man," Brokk mused. "I hear the labor is hard and you can't have more than a few good years left in you."

"I had hoped in the weeks following your embarrassing defeat at the hand of my army, you would have changed tactics," Remmel retorted, spite dripping from every word.

Brokk wanted to slap him but he abstained. Instead, he decided to continue past his captive to don his combat garb. "I hope they pay what you're worth," he muttered.

CHAPTER THREE

After shedding her cotton clothes and taking a bath, Tamara was dressed by the two handmaids in a flowing blue dress that shimmered in the ever-present sunlight. She felt beautiful, but she was just an object. A tool to be used for the outlet of a man's energy. Nothing more.

Tamara longed for the days of good old Red and his band of mercenaries. Red viewed her as a tool too, but he also treated her like family. She didn't mind being a tool if that meant she was useful and cared for, but an object without worth was a fate worse than death and she wished she had been given the chance to die fighting just like Red on that ship all those years ago. She thought about Red often, wondering if he'd made it. Wondering if someday, Red and his filthy white tank top would show up at Orno's door demanding Tamara back. A pipe dream, yes, but something worth holding on to.

It was dusk on the planet and despite the fact that Charoth didn't rotate, it did wobble. The north-south rocking of the planet shifted the sun in the sky between morning and night over a fifteen-hour span.

Thus, the sun would move to the top of the mountain after fifteen hours and then travel to the sea over the next fifteen hours.

As the handmaids fussed over the back of Tamara's dress, she gazed lazily out of the window towards the mountains where the sun presently hovered. Those beautiful mountains; the very ones that had thrust her into this present predicament. But they were worth staring at all the same; maybe even worth escaping to. *Bide your time*, she thought. *One day, you'll be free to explore those mountains.*

"Not like that," hissed one of the women. Tamara heard a slap of flesh against flesh as the two bickered back and forth.

"Stop being so childish," exclaimed the other. "I'll do it, just get me that pin."

The first woman sighed and Tamara could feel fingers gently running up and down her spine as they worked to tailor the dress to fit Tamara's slender figure. The wound on her back had been treated in mere minutes and her skin was entirely healed. *The benefits of modern medicine*, she thought. *He can destroy a body only to put it back together again.*

Her master was a man of peculiar tastes and instead of simply using the female slaves for his pleasure, he preferred to dine with them first. Tamara suspected he secretly abhorred himself and wanted the women to like him, not as their slave master but as a man they would like to befriend. Of course, none of the women did; instead, she and the others despised him all the more. He was too gutless to treat them like the objects they were and too dull for any of them to be interested in his friendship. Her master's loneliness, she suspected was well deserved, and instead of finding real friends or changing who he was, he surrounded himself with servants to tell him how great he was. A man to be pitied; a man to be hated.

"There," said one of the women from behind. "Don't you look beautiful? Master will be so pleased," she exclaimed with glee.

"Now if we can just fix this flower," said the other. Tamara could feel the woman gently tugging on her hair and she detected the scent of a tarib, a beautiful red flower with an orange stem and large petals. There was no mirror in her dressing room, only a window carved out of the tan stone that the rest of the home had been made of but she knew what was happening. The master didn't like to see the metallic crown that he had surgeons screw into her scalp. He liked the benefits but pretended to be blissfully ignorant of the fact that he kept her there against her will. His maids busily worked to cover it up by weaving and braiding her hair around it and then using flowers as an extra layer. He was a gutless and peculiar man indeed.

A gentle breeze pushed through the north-facing window and Tamara allowed herself to close her eyes as the gentle fingers continued to work on her hair. Footsteps alerted her to open them again but instead of a visitor, she realized that someone had left while the other continued her work. She had moved to Tamara's shoulders now, sewing the seams of her dress tight against her skin.

Tamara's eyes were heavy from the work and she wanted to drift again but something called to her from the window. Suddenly, a silver dart streaked across the northern sky and caught Tamara's attention. The spaceport was to the west and she would never be able to see ships taking off and landing at the spaceport out of her current window, especially not facing the mountains. As she watched, Tamara became certain it was a vessel because on several occasions it slowed and changed directions, only to accelerate again. *But why would a ship venture to the far end of the habitable zone?*

Eventually, the craft disappeared from view, hidden against the mountains to the north. Footsteps again came into the room. "Dinner is ready," said the woman. "The master will have you seated now."

* * *

The dining room in the master's villa was on the second floor of the stone structure and possessed its own private balcony that wrapped around the entirety of the villa. The room itself was open to the air and a gentle breeze on a warm night pushed past stone pillars that held the roof above their heads.

Tamara sat upright in her seat and waited for her master's arrival, at which point she would stand and bow, giving him the honor he believed he deserved. While she waited, she allowed herself to gaze out at the mountains, the barriers between civilization and chaos and the gates of her freedom. Instead of escape, she wondered what she had witnessed earlier. Curiosity drove her mad and she yearned for another day in space; for an opportunity to travel the cosmos with Red and his mercenaries.

Most of all, she yearned to sense the elements again. To be able to feel the atoms in the sandstone, the raw emotions of a friend, and to be able to manipulate the heat of the fire. To muzzle her senses with the metallic crown was like taking the gift of sight away from a person. It was cruel and painful, but what was she to do. *Bide your time, Tamara,* she could hear Red telling her. *Bide your time and strike when you're strong.*

Torn from her thoughts was the announcement of her master. She stood and the same shrewd man she had been with mere months before entered and provided a hand for her to kiss. "My lord," she said, bowing and pressing her lips to his hand. It was as soft and as feminine as the women that braided her hair. She suddenly felt scorn for the man welling up inside her; scorn and hatred.

"Ah, my beautiful Tamara," he exclaimed, looking her up and down. "It is a beautiful dress they picked for you tonight, is it not?"

"It is my lord," she replied, eager to sit down and be on with the evening. Her master was dressed in a long thin robe that opened to reveal an ornate green tunic with a high collar. She'd never seen such a thing and thought it looked ridiculous. Making his dress even more absurd were the clashing gray pants under his white robe that flared at the knees and hugged his ankles. Certainly not something a man with any sense would wear.

He paid no attention to her eyes and instead spun her around to look at her open back, touching her sun baked skin with his soft, unlabored hand. "A beautiful dress indeed," he said again.

At last, the greeting was over and her master seated himself across from her. The table had been decorated with two candles made of hoffo wax and a platter of bread and fruit was sprawled out in front of her. Her mouth salivated and her stomach growled but she couldn't touch a morsel until he had sampled all of the food first while her own hunger grew to an intolerable level.

He was in a talkative mood tonight and to her great dismay, pushed his empty plate from his chest and let out a sigh. "My dear Tamara," he started, pausing to look around at the extravagant food choices laid out before him. "Do you remember the day we first met?"

Did she remember? How could she forget standing on a pedestal for all of Charoth to gawk at? Men touched her and examined her features. Filthy slave buyers shoved their fingers into her mouth to examine her teeth while others knocked sticks against her knees to see if she was sturdy. For days she stood in that sun, only to be brought in after she had collapsed from exhaustion, rehabilitated by the modern medicine she wished didn't exist, and sent back out into the sun to bake for another twelve hours.

She certainly remembered. It is a strange sensation to realize that the fear of being bought by slavers has been conquered by the dread of standing any longer. That the desire for death outgrew the desire to continue living in the destitute world of Charoth. When she saw him, she knew he had picked her to purchase. He had returned to her three times previously, questioning the slaver and examining her records. She was relieved to move on with her sentence and into a home with someone that had spent money for her.

"Yes, lord," she responded, eyes cast to the table ensuring to never make eye contact with her master.

"I remember too. You were terrified in that market, but look how far you've come. I've always thought you were a great addition to the team," he said, gesturing beyond the open pillars towards the slave quarters below.

She knew where this was going and steeled herself for the catch. There was always a catch and she never knew why he felt the need to give motivational speeches to his slaves.

"But," he continued. "I can't have you looking towards that mountain. That's what Fielio told me you were doing. Were you looking towards that mountain? Were you thinking of escaping?"

"No, lord," was her reply, but sensing the need to elaborate she quickly did so. "The dust was in my eyes... and the wind. I was simply shielding myself. It was just a mistake, lord." She hoped he would accept her explanation.

He didn't. "We can't have you running off, Tamara." His words faked concern but dripped contempt. "You wouldn't survive out there, you know?" He paused and surveyed the food again. "Let's put this behind us and eat, shall we?"

Relief flooded into her body and her saliva ran wild inside her mouth. But she wouldn't get the chance to taste even one morsel. Rushing through the door came the buffoon that had whipped her earlier, red-faced and panting, but this time he carried a rifle. "Orno, visitors, warriors, they demand to see you at once."

Her master jumped to his feet. "What? Right now? Are they downstairs?"

Taking a breath, the man nodded. "Yes, lord. They're waiting downstairs."

"Well," he said, pausing to gather his thoughts. "Bring the guests up. There's plenty of food and I'm sure they'll appreciate the view as much as I do." He grinned and Tamara knew he meant her, sending shudders down her neck. "Put the girl in the corner," he hissed at one of his maids. "Make sure they can see her form."

Moments after being moved to the corner, Tamara's legs trembled as three very large men entered the dining hall. The first had light golden skin and towered over her master. His broad shoulders and square jaw were offset only by the size of the legs that carried him. He wore black clothes and a rifle of some sort hung at his fingertips, dangling on a sling off his shoulder. On either side stood two red-skinned men, nearly as large and just as wide. Hair covered their bodies and their jaws, the lower bigger than the upper, caused thick white teeth to be exposed beyond them. They too were clothed in black and armed with rifles.

Orno jumped to meet their guests. "I'm Orno, please, sit and relax. While I'm surprised by your visit, I'm grateful you've come so far from the city to meet with me."

The men ignored him, instead looking around the room. Tamara suspected they were searching for threats. Three of Orno's thugs were also in the room, but they looked tiny compared to the men that now occupied her former space. But there was something else. Something Tamara hadn't felt in a long time. As soon as she saw the golden man, her head throbbed and tingled, but it didn't hurt. Suddenly, she could sense everything around him. She felt and heard his heartbeat. She could explore his skin and the elements that composed the clothes covering his body.

She suddenly sensed the room around her too, not as she had with her eyes or her hands, but with her mind. All of it, down to the very elements that beamed and beckoned her to call them. A flood of relief filled her. She could sense again. She felt alive, rejuvenated, filled!

Finally, the golden man spoke and each word that flowed from his mouth formed a visible ladder for her to climb on and dance around as his voice sent sound waves up and out through the room. "Orno, it is nice to meet you. I'm Brokk." The man paused, but something on Orno's face led him to continue. Unalarmed, he moved forward and pulled out a chair. "I'm grateful for you providing the food on such short notice," he continued. "We're new here and looking for friends.

My ship crashed near the mountain, we had mechanical issues. Do you think you could lend us a hand?"

The golden man lied. Orno couldn't sense it, but Tamara could. Suddenly she was perplexed. The words that came from his mouth were red but were coated in blue and green as well. He lied, but she sensed it was for some unknown purpose. Some positioning or strategy that was yet to be learned. Orno took a seat as well and a pleased-looking grin coated his previously perplexed persona. "I'm grateful you've found me first. From where do you come?" he asked.

Tamara could suddenly sense Orno's words as well, as if the golden man amplified everything around her. His presence sent a tingling sensation down her spine and she could hardly contain herself, but she had to. She had to wait a little longer.

Brokk ignored him, instead shoveling a handful of greltins into his mouth. "These are your men?" Brokk asked, waving a sharp utensil around at the three overseers standing on the balcony.

"I have many more than just those three," Orno replied, "But yes, those are my men."

"How many more?" Brokk asked. The question worried Tamara. It was too forward, too probing, too carefree. The red disappeared and instead, his words were black, bloodthirsty, manipulative. This golden-skinned man wasn't here on accident. He was looking for something, but Tamara was too overjoyed to consider the danger. She felt as light as a feather, entirely sustained by the sudden return of her senses.

Orno again didn't notice Brokk's intentions. If only he hadn't thought so little of Tamara, she could have helped him. She had found a new master now, she would reach out to him. "Perhaps fifty," he said slyly as if the man that made his own men look small would shake. "Are these you came with, are they it?" Orno asked.

"Hardly," Brokk responded with a growl, once again looking around the room. His eyes met Tamara's and lingered for just a moment before moving on and eventually resting back on Orno. He noticed her, but not enough and a sudden urgency gripped her. Tamara knew she had her chance. She reached out with her mind and touched him gently, moving his chin back to her eyes.

Like a doll on strings, Brokk lifted his head and fixed his eyes on hers. *Good,* she thought, cupping his head in her hands. *Notice me and I am yours.* But she sensed tension. More than she had ever felt before and the man with the golden skin ripped his eyes from hers and returned his glare to Orno. *No!* She screamed in her mind. This was her chance. *Get him back.* She focused, grabbing him with her immaterial self but feeling only darkness.

"You trade slaves?" he asked, motioning with a knife he had picked up from the table towards Tamara.

"I buy them for work and sell them once they are no longer useful. But I don't trade them per-say. This farm provides the wine to most restaurants in the city. I need workers and occasional company at night. They do well."

Brokk scoffed but Orno pretended not to notice. His eyes were on making money. Tamara wasn't so certain these men had come to do business. She wondered how to be more forceful, how to get his attention. She might never get this chance again.

"You should do your research when you buy a slave," Brokk said.

Orno suddenly looked caught off guard. He looked around the room and stammered, trying to find the words. "Excuse me," he finally managed to say. "My slaves have all served me perfectly well. They even prepared this meal you are devouring."

Orno was simply too dull. Brokk had known immediately. As soon as she reached out and touched him he knew what she was. Her heart leapt in her chest. It had worked.

"How much for that one?" Brokk asked, pointing again at her.

"Oh, she isn't for sale." Her master responded. "She wouldn't serve you any purpose. It's only escape that she thinks about and she doesn't work very hard," Orno lied. He paused to examine her, staring into her eyes as if to teach her a lesson for her mistake earlier in the day. "I have some strong men that I would be happy to sell you. They work hard and would surely help on your journey."

Brokk pushed his chair back abruptly and rose to his feet, giving a nod to his guards. Tamara was startled, she hadn't sensed his sudden action like she should have. The man was masking himself from her. She watched as the two red-skinned guards he entered with faced Orno's slavers. They didn't raise their weapons but they startled the bodyguards and put them on edge. She was in the middle of a stand-off, if not announced, certainly spoken with their body language.

Brokk looked at Tamara, suddenly his own eyes flared and she could sense him again, all of him. She felt his hatred and his pain. She sensed his longing for something deep. She felt the power and energy in his body. But most of all, she knew what he was going to do, and she was suddenly terrified. Terrified, but excited. Excited and ready.

"You don't have fifty men, do you Orno?"

Orno rose to his feet as well, but before he could speak Brokk silenced him by raising his finger. Awestruck, Orno watched as Brokk walked over to Tamara and placed his hand on her shoulder. Instantly, her senses erupted. She not only could feel Brokk and the people in the room, but she could sense everyone on the farm. She heard and felt the beating hearts of dozens of slaves and she could not only feel them, she could hear and touch them too.

How the golden man knew, she did not know, but he squeezed her shoulder and whispered "focus" into her ear, bringing her back into the room. Then, Brokk addressed Orno.

"This one is special, you fool," he said, sending Orno's mouth to the floor and his eyes wide. "In a few seconds, you and the cowards in this room are going to feel extreme pain under your skin. It will be your blood boiling. Then, I am going to take your farm and your slaves with it."

Orno wanted to speak, he even tried to, but he couldn't. Not anymore. Tamara reached inside the hearts of Orno and his overseers and turned their blood from warm to hot and from hot to boiling. Orno screamed, but Tamara couldn't hear him; all she felt was joy. She could sense again and each high-pitched note that erupted from the men agonizing around her fluttered throughout the room like butterflies in an open field.

Turning up the heat, she allowed her spirit to climb each note until she was hovering not just above her body, but above the entire villa. From her new vantage point, she could feel dozens of hearts pounding below. She wanted all of them and she no longer had to ask permission. They were hers for the taking. As with the four in the room, musical waves burst upwards as she heated their blood, using their hearts as ovens and boiling the liquid through their skin. Their screams meant nothing to her, it was only her joy, her elation that mattered.

Then, there was silence and it was finished. A light breeze pushed in through the balcony and Tamara returned to the room with a newfound sense of freedom. Her slavers lay on the floor unmoving and she could no longer sense their life. Orno's mouth hung open, forever frozen in agony. *He deserved worse.*

Brokk spun her around to face him and she eagerly submitted herself to his grip. Gently, he pulled the flowers out of her hair and unbraided it to reveal the metallic crown embedded in her skull. Removing a tool from his belt, he unscrewed the contraption one bolt at a time. Tamara wanted to faint from the pain, but she dug deep, not in herself, but inside Brokk and once inside, she found all the strength she would ever need.

"You're going to be very happy with us," Brokk said with a smile. "Let's get you to your new home."

I hope you've enjoyed this preview. You can buy Rogue Fleet on Amazon or at your local bookstore today!